THE PICKLE QUEEN

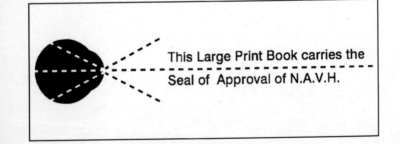

This Large Print Book carries the Seal of Approval of N.A.V.H.

THE PICKLE QUEEN

A CROSSROADS CAFÉ NOVELLA

DEBORAH SMITH

THORNDIKE PRESS
A part of Gale, Cengage Learning

Farmington Hills, Mich • San Francisco • New York • Waterville, Maine
Meriden, Conn • Mason, Ohio • Chicago

GALE
CENGAGE Learning®

LIBRARY OF CONGRESS CATALOGING-IN-PUBLICATION DATA

Smith, Deborah, 1955–
    The pickle queen : a Crossroads Café novella / by Deborah Smith. — Large print edition.
        pages ; cm. — (Thorndike Press large print clean reads) (MacBrides ; #2)
    ISBN 978-1-4104-7029-4 (hardcover) — ISBN 1-4104-7029-6 (hardcover)
    1. Families—North Carolina—Fiction. 2. Appalachian Region—Fiction.
    3. Large type books. I. Title.
PS3569.M5177P525 2014
813'.54—dc23   2014010294

Published in 2014 by arrangement with BelleBooks, Inc.

Printed in Mexico
1 2 3 4 5 6 7 18 17 16 15 14

THE PICKLE QUEEN

The Crossroads Cove

and right next door is Free Wheeler also Turtleville

Up there, Canada, the North Pole, and such

The Little Finn River Valley & town of Tearmann Virginia

Kentucky

Tennessee

Great Smoky Mtns. National Forest

Us (North Carolina)

Georgia

Alabama

South Carolina

Asheville & just across the river, West Asheville

Ireland, Scotland, Wales, England & Whatever else

Florida, Cuba, & other hot places

The rest of the South, Texas, desert mountains, Hollywood

Delta's Family Recipe

LARD

"The Mysterious Ways" —

Notebook in Cobbs

THE FAMILIES

THE FAMILIES OF
THE CROSSROADS COVE
(Also Free Wheeler, Asheville, Tearmann &
the Little Finn River Valley)

Whittlespoons-
Delta Nettie Whittlespoon: related to Netties, Jeffersons, and most of the other old families of Appalachian western North Carolina; one of the Nettie "biscuit witches," and owner of the famous CROSSROADS CAFÉ; her husband Pike Whittlespoon (Sheriff of Jefferson County); Pike's brother, Joe ("Santa Joe")

Netties-
Mary Eve Nettie; Emma Nettie (aka Rose Dooly); Cathy Deen (a Nettie on her maternal side), actress, married to Tom Mitternich, architect, of New York; their daughters, Cora and Ivy, and their twin sons, Ben and

Ned; Jane Eve Nettie MacBride (mother of Gus, Gabby, Tal, grandmother of Tal's daughter, Eve)

Wakefields-

Augustus Wakefield, early 1900's, built some of Asheville's most iconic buildings and homes, wiped out MacBrides and others up in the Little Finn River Valley during the 1930 moonshine war, a ploy to gain mining rights. He stole Free Wheeler from Arlo Claptraddle, aka Sam Osserman, in 1940's for revenge over losing Emma to him but also for mining rights; William Wakefield, son of Augustus, lost a key Free Wheeler mining right to Mary Eve Nettie in a poker game, 1960's; Thomas Wakefield, son of William, philantrophist, preservationist, inherited surface rights to Free Wheeler from William; E.W. Wakefield, older brother of Thomas, main heir to Wakefield Mining and Land Development, inherited remaining rights to Free Wheeler; Denoto and Quincy Wakefield, daughters of E.W. Wakefield; Jay Wakefield, son of Thomas Wakefield, cousin of Denoto and Quincy

MacBrides-

Caillin MacBride, only known survivor of the 1930 moonshine war; her great nephew,

Stewart MacBride; Jane Eve Nettie Mac-
Bride, his wife; their children, Groucho
(Gus), Greta (Gabby), and Tallulah Mac-
Bride, aka the kitchen charmer, the pickle
queen, and the biscuit witch; Tal's daughter,
Eve; Tal's fiancé, Dr. Doug Firth, DVM

Bonavendiers-
Will Bonavendier; his sister, the Reverend
Bonnie Bonavendier; descendants of a
Louisiana family related to Wakefields and
MacBrides through old connections. Heirs
to the Little Finn River Valley.

Part One

Gabby
2012
Pickles Are Our Friends, Not Just Our Food

Pickles are mentioned in the Bible. Cleopatra ate them as a beauty regimen. Shakespeare put them in his plays. Mason designed jars for bottling them. So did Ball. Did Mason and Ball fight over the *King of the Pickle Jars* title? I don't know. I did know this much: I used pickles to keep fear, pride, and my love of Jay Wakefield behind a door I would not risk opening again. Even now.

My Pre-Christmas Lecture from Tal

They called *me* the bossy one and Tal the sweet one, but in the past two weeks, since Tal left New York for cousin Delta's cove high in the mountains above Asheville, North Carolina, my and Gus's baby sister had transformed into an Appalachian *hoo-doo* woman. For the first time in her life, thanks to Scottish veterinarian Dr. Douglas Firth, our biscuit witch was in love, with extra butter on top. She now claimed to have the all-seeing vision of a spirit bear, the earth-mother insights of a country-western singer, and the we-must-return-to-our-roots fervor of a trout swimming up-stream to spawn.

I'm not certain mountain trout do that, but if they do, Tallulah Bankhead MacBride had become their honorary swimming in-structor.

She emailed me before Christmas, not knowing I was in a Los Angeles courtroom fighting to prove I hadn't stolen five million dollars from my movie-star partner.

Dear Big Sister,

There's something going on between you and Jay Wakefield. Admit it. Not just from when we were kids. When he came to the Cove to make that cold-blooded offer about hiring us to work for him at Free Wheeler (when he knows we're the rightful heirs!), my food angels couldn't get a good grip on his secrets and pain. But now that Doug and I are lovers, my angels have expanded their menu! The

14

same thing happened when Eve was born. I'm full of aromas and everyone around me is a glory-full meal of spiritual flavors!

It's true what Mama always said: It tastes good to be alive!

So here's what my foodie angels are telling me: Jay has turned into baking chocolate. He's got barely enough sugar left to qualify as "bittersweet." He's desperate for more sugar. Just like when we were kids, only much, much worse. For love. Trust. Family. For you. You, Gabby. You. He needs you like cocoa butter needs vanilla.

I know I told you to let me and Doug handle him. I told you not to listen when Delta was egging you on with all that talk about, "Go after him, just remember you can catch more flies with honey than with vinegar, Pickle Queen."

But I was wrong. You need to go after him. Come here. Come home.

Where we were born. Where we belong.

I came home. Now you and Gus come home, too.

Love, Tal

"The hearing's about to start." My lawyer

laid her hand on my shoulder. You know things are bad when your attorney keeps patting you.

My senses filled with avocado and lemon. The lawyer's safe place.

Tal's foodie angels brought her visions of baked goods. Mine brought brine, peppers, spices, tastes that bit back. If my chances of walking away without being charged with embezzlement got any worse, my lawyer was going to turn into guacamole.

I closed the cover on my phone and stood.

I wasn't going back to North Carolina. Or back to Jay. Not ever. The sweet boy I remembered was lost inside a bitter man. He'd become what he'd once hated most. A Wakefield.

Jay
Wakefield, MacBride, Nettie, Whittlespoon
Atop the Rock of Ages
1989

Love is an open vein in a mountain of granite rock. Elemental. Gabby and I were bonded under pressure, sealed in the earth, surfaced by heat, crystalized by fire. Like sands through the hour glass, these are the days of the lies we survived. Our Wakefield-MacBride legacy started deep inside the rock of ages.

Sand. Silica. Silicon Dioxide. SiO2. Known since ancient times. Quartz. The most common working-class rock on the planet. The bedrock under the mattress of the Blue Ridge Mountains that cover our part of North Carolina.

My great-grandfather Augustus didn't know or care about the minerals under the surface of Free Wheeler when he bankrupted Arlo Claptraddle by buying his competition and driving bicycle prices into the ground; Augustus just wanted revenge for Arlo rescuing, hiding, and winning the heart of Augustus's extraordinary cook, a young mountain beauty named Emma Nettie. Back in the 1940s, Emma was on Great-Grandfather's short list for the next opening in his long list of mistresses. Her lack of interest in the position didn't stop him from locking her in a room at his Asheville mansion until she came to her senses.

She escaped and headed back to her family near the Crossroads Cove, only to be tracked by Augustus's hired security men. She found refuge in the strange world of inventor and bicycle maker Arlo, whose

Clapper Motion Machines were built in the community he invented with all the whimsy of a cross between Walt Disney and a post-Victorian Mad Hatter.

For the next ten years, she lived with, worked with, loved and inspired Arlo, going under the name Rose Dooley. He designed a bike for her. He adored her. He would have married her, if he hadn't been separated from a wife in his wealthy circles. Divorce wasn't an option. The paperwork would have exposed Emma's identity.

Eventually, in the 1950s, Great-Grandfather found her. You don't take a woman from a Wakefield. You don't take anything from a Wakefield. Not and live to talk about it.

So that, friends, is the short version of how Free Wheeler, an abandoned and haunted bicycle village near the cove, came to be the property, *in perpetuum,* of Wakefields, to serve as a warning to anyone who ever thought about crossing us again.

Like putting a head of your enemy on a stake outside your castle walls.

Now, that head had become surprisingly valuable.

Fifty feet beneath Dad's Birkenstock sandals and Uncle E.W.'s tasseled loafers lay a vein of Carolina quartz so pure it could be pulverized into sand as white as bleached cotton. Wakefield Mining and Land Development considered quartz a throwaway. Scrape the valuable feldspar and mica out of the ground, separate the quartz that ran through it, sell the quartz sand to golf courses. It made those eye-popping sugar-white sand traps people saw on television at the Masters Tournament.

Until a little worldwide revolution called the silicon chip came along. North Carolina quartz became the gourmet truffle of silica, worth fortunes.

"I inherited the surface access, right?" E.W. said loudly, snapping his fingers in the thick summer air.

One of his attorneys stepped forward with a document, as if the mere appearance of a piece of paper was drama enough for the wild and isolated setting. "You know that. It's a standard easement."

Thick blue-green mountains rose around Free Wheeler's weedy main street and sad, haunted buildings — all that remained of Arlo Claptraddle's bicycle shops, his factory and the little town he built for the workers who became his family. A magical mountain village where people rode their Claptraddle bicycles on pretty paths to the cottages he built all through the valley, all the way to the fancy pavement of the Asheville Trace and into the Crossroads Cove, where the Jeffersons and Whittlespoons and Netties and other old families filled their bicycle baskets with fine corn whiskey; and where the friendly roadside farmhouse of Delta Whittlespoon's grandmother would one day become Delta's famous Crossroads Café Diner.

"I have the right to dig up as much of this God-forsaken piece of Nothing as need be," my uncle insisted, as his private security men stepped forward with folded arms. Uncle E.W. was hated by a lot of people; nothing new for us Wakefields, but did he really believe I, Dad and Lawyer George were going to jump him? Behind him and his army of suits waited bulldozers and graders ridden by men in yellow hardhats. We'd be bulldozed before we got half a chance to attack.

"Go home, Elba," Dad said. "We're rich. We don't need more money. We need to keep what's left of our souls."

"My soul wants progress, Baby Brother. Job creation. Tax money going to the coffers of our great state. And raw materials for the technology revolution that will keep our great nation at the forefront of . . ."

"Save your rhetoric for interviews and

press releases. You want to own every mining property in this part of the state. You've put most of your investments in off-shore accounts, you've bribed regulators to look the other way and bought politicians and strong-armed activists. It's a family tradition, I know. But this is one place where our family name is not going to be attached to the wholesale destruction and desecration of a historic site, not to mention a pristine natural environment."

"I've been patient long enough, Tommy. There's not a damned thing worth preserving here. It's just a bunch of old buildings in the middle of the woods, full of junked bicycle parts and cobwebs."

"It should be given to Arlo's heirs."

"There are none."

"That's debatable. Emma had a daughter . . ."

"No proof of paternity. And it wouldn't matter anyway. Grandfather's will says this property stays in our family. If you try to hand it off to strangers, you forfeit it to me."

"I understand that, Brother. That's why I'm going to protect it. I have no choice."

"I'll give you twenty percent of the net profit from the quarry I develop. You can't legally stop me, Tommy." He shook the document. "By God, I've got mining rights.

Those include the access right. An easement to come onto this property and dig."

I looked up at Dad with my fists clenched in the pockets of my khakis. Did even God know that E.W. Wakefield was the majority stockholder and CEO of one of the biggest mining companies in the southeast? That Wakefields had been gouging fortunes out of these mountains since the late eighteen hundreds?

Dad looked so tired. He'd inherited Free Wheeler from their father as a throwaway gift to a sickly second son. E.W. got the good stuff — the mining rights. Dad got the useless, pretty surface. Dad wanted it that way.

Dad leaned on his cane. A lifetime of type 1 diabetes had taken a toll on the nerve endings in his feet. He was a tall skinny pine tree pushed sideways by an ice storm. I stood as close beside him as I could without impugning his dignity by shoving a shoulder into his hip to hold him up. I was tall for eleven, but he was the size of the Olympian giants. In my eyes, at least.

"Elba," he said in an elegant uplands drawl, "couldn't you just once do the righteous thing?"

"Arlo Claptraddle nearly killed Grandfather. He assaulted him. The bastard died in prison. Rightfully so. I've got no qualms."

"This place should be preserved, regardless," Dad said.

"Sir?" Dad's assistant whispered. He had been listening intently on a satellite phone he clutched to one ear.

"Yes, George?" Dad looked tired. I leaned into his shadow. I loved him more than breathing. Even more than he loved me. And he loved me even more than he loved old buildings, history, doing the right thing, comic books, and honesty.

Lawyer George — my nickname for George Avery — whispered to Dad, his thinning blond hair ruffled and sweaty, his open golf shirt showing a slight stain where his wife hadn't quite smudged out the burp-up from their baby. Dad could afford an entourage; he just didn't like the idea. "You're better backup than ten lawyers and a Rock 'Em Sock 'Em Robot plus three Godzillas and a team of X-Men," he always said to George and me.

George finished whispering. Dad looked at E.W. "Give me five minutes, Elba. I have proof that your access rights belong to someone else."

Uncle E.W.'s lawyers did everything except roll their eyes and laugh. One of them stepped forward and handed E.W. a folder.

He held it up triumphantly. "Court order," he said. He waved the folder at the men behind him.

A bulldozer rumbled.

My stomach clenched. I looked up at Dad's gaunt face. Unzipping the hip pack I always carried, I pulled out a small bottle of orange juice. "Cap'n, it's time to re-fuel your jet pack."

George gave me an approving thumbs-up. "Sir, Junior Commander Jay is making an excellent suggestion. Let's conference in the shade of a tree and —"

Dad cut us off with a gently-raised hand. He tilted his head, listening. In the distance, along a rutted trail that ran back through the woods toward the place people called the Crossroads Cove, came the sound of a car engine. Dad smiled. "The Rebels are here early. I knew they'd make it." He winked at me. "Darth Elba doesn't stand a chance."

A brown and white SUV rumbled into view. Muddy with big tires, fog lights and blue lights on top and a Jefferson County Sheriff's Department seal on each side. A tall young deputy in khaki pants and a short-sleeve shirt stepped out; from the front passenger seat popped a sexy brown-haired woman in tight blue jeans and a tank top. She carried a big paper bag with twine handles. It bulged with mysterious contents. Her eyes crinkled when she saw the Us Against Them scene. She liked bad odds, I decided.

The deputy opened the SUV's back door. A little old man in overalls climbed out, and the deputy helped him put on a dark formal coat over the overalls. Then the woman took his arm to steady him. With her acting as his prop, the three of them headed our way.

The warm June air brought a scent to me. Bread, buttery, rich. The woman smiled down at me as if she knew I was hypnotized. She reached inside the bag. "Here. You must be Jay." Her mountain drawl was as soulful as the aroma around her.

I glanced from her to Dad. He nodded. I took the plastic-wrapped biscuit she offered. It was bigger than a grown man's fist and still warm from the oven. The aroma went through the shield of my skin and up my arm. I'd been biscuitized.

"Delta, Deputy. I present Jayson Wakefield. Jay, this is Deputy Pike Whittlespoon and Mrs. Whittlespoon."

"Very pleased to meet you," I said. My hand felt heavy and happy, holding the magical biscuit.

Deputy Whittlespoon cupped my shoulder

in a fatherly way, then stepped aside. "Thomas, this is Judge Rescule Solbert. Been retired a few decades but still sits on the bench once a month over in Turtleville —"

"See here, now, you conniving Wakefield horn-rimming rock hound!" the ancient Jefferson County judge said loudly, shuffling toward Uncle E.W. Delta set her bag of biscuits down and hustled along beside him, though his agitated quickstep seemed pretty secure. He dug a veined hand inside his coat and pulled out a piece of paper, which he held up between wizened fingers. "Nineteen sixty-nine! The Dog House. We called it a 'private club' to keep the preachers and the church ladies and the law of a damn dry county satisfied. Jack Farmer and his daughters ran it out of what had been the old Little Finn River Road Toll Store. Had a coupla TVs, a pool table, some card tables, a bar, a juke box, dart boards. Had a cooler full of good beer and a locker full of better liquor." He shook the paper under E.W.'s nose. "Little Finn River Road. You Wakefields know that name. You murderin' bunch of thieves. Wiped out all those Mac-Brides back in the thirties, turned that whole valley into a tomb . . . your devil granddaddy, rot in hell, Augustus Wakefield —"

The security men leapt forward. So did Delta. She planted herself between the judge and his goons, her hands on her hips.

Her husband called out, "Don't hurt 'em, pussycat."

E.W. sliced the air. "Old man, say what you've got to say." Uncle E.W. drew himself up to his full six-four, disdaining the withered old mountain judge and his colorful details of the local road house. "Is there a point to this?"

Judge Solbert grinned at him from behind Delta's freckled shoulder, showing a fake-perfect bottom denture but no upper teeth. *Judge Bulldog.*

"The point, Elba Wyatt Wakefield, is that I was there the night your daddy wagered this property's digging rights in a poker game. And he lost. I witnessed the transaction and signed it."

Uncle E.W.'s mouth drew up in prune. "I assume you're waving a copy of that so-called wager?"

"Tee hee, you bet, you greedy bastard. Go back to Asheville and figure out how to gouge fortunes out of these hills somewhere else." He shoved the paper into my uncle's hand. "Mary Eve Nettie won the easement in that game. Won it fair and square. I knew Wakefields can't be trusted, so I got a lot more witnesses' signatures besides my own, that night."

E.W. glanced at the paper as if it repelled him, then flung it at his lawyers. They huddled over it like crows ganging up on a snake. One look at their combined stare of dismay said the snake was a big one.

E.W. shoved past Delta and the judge, thrusting his finger at Dad as he advanced. "That goddamned right is useless to who-ever this Mary Eve Nettie is! I'll buy it from her!"

"She's my cousin," Delta called, "and she knew what it was worth, and she didn't want this place destroyed. She said so until her dying day."

"Then she left the access right to an heir."

"That would be me," Delta said. "And you can go to hell. I'm keeping it." She looked at Dad. "No offense, but it's better off with me than with you, cause if I get 'accidentally' dead thanks to your brother, a whole of pack of hillbillies will wage war on him until the end of time. You can't beat that."

Dad smiled. "No, I can't." He nodded to George. "Explain the legal fine points to E.W. and his team, George."

Lawyer George puffed out his chest in a way that said, *Yes I got my degree at No Name U instead of Duke, while working as a waiter at a Red Lobster, so what?* He rattled off a long explanation of the current status for a vague mining right passed down by inheritance from Augustus to William then parlayed out of William's ownership via a poker game twenty years ago, now owned by Delta Whittlespoon.

When he finished, Judge Solbert cackled. "That, fellows, is ten-dollar lawyer talk for 'Y'all are up shit creek on this one.' "

E.W. exploded. "That access right is mine, and I *will* regain it, Tommy, even if I have to twist your arm or break your neck or find your weak spot I will, and if you get in my way again —"

"You've never frightened me," Dad said, which I didn't doubt, because Dad believed in guardian spirits, in angels, and said that powers bigger than any of us had made the stars and the earth, the rocks of ages, the eternity of love. E.W. and all his minions couldn't beat that. But Dad's voice had a thready sound I recognized. Probably a drop in his blood sugar. "Don't even try," Dad started, then halted.

Lawyer George grabbed his arm. I tossed the shoulder pack and he unzipped it.

"Dad, drink some OJ!"

I got between Dad and E.W., who continued to head straight toward us, finger jabbing, face furious. A rush of things happened: security men running up, Deputy Whittlespoon jumping in the middle, but I focused on E.W.'s stomach. I was tall for my age, so when I drew back a fist it was level with my uncle's breastbone. Because I went to an alternative education school (the courses included Spiritual Wealth, Leadership Ethics, and Community Living,) my sports were also alternative, meaning yoga and non-violent tai chi.

I opted for something out of Dad's collection of Kung Fu movies.

I jabbed my uncle in the soft spot below the ribcage. Solar plexus. He clutched his chest and went down.

Behind me, so did Dad.

"Hold his hand, sweetie, hold his hand and pray," Delta Whittlespoon whispered in my ear as Dad died. Her arms were around me from behind, her cheek was pressed close to mine, but we both sat there helplessly as Deputy Whittlespoon performed CPR and Lawyer George talked intensely to Dad's cardiologist in Asheville. Dad's big, thin hand was clenched so tight inside both of mine I thought he was holding on, but it was me doing all the holding. He seemed to be looking up at me but also at the trees and the mountains, the funny old buildings of Free Wheeler, loving me and all of that.

Take care of it for us, Jay.

I will. I swear.

He saw farther into the heart of the air, the Appalachians, the universe, until finally he got so far away he couldn't hear me begging him to stay.

Uncle E.W. stood off to one side, holding his stomach, not even crying.

Watching me, the heir.

Gabby
Smoke Got in Their Eyes

The day I first met Jay I was armed for trouble and in a mood to whack strangers. Again. Five sneaky neighbor kids, three street bums and two dogs had tried to steal food from the front-yard smokers. It wasn't like they couldn't get free handouts. A big sandwich board right by the front walkway said, If You Can't Pay Today, You Can Pay Later. Right beside that sign hung a big iron cow bell. All a person had to do was clang it. Me or Gus would come around from the back yard, bringing take-out boxes, and we'd fill them up, no questions asked.

31

Only dogs and Daddy's buddies in the police department got a pass on the clanging rule. Nobody else.

Mama — Jane Eve Nettie MacBride — said God gave her and her children — me, Tal and Gus — the gift of food magic as our special way to offer love to others. To feed the heartsick and needy, to soothe the dispirited. After all, who knew when we might be serving up a buffet to an angel, unawares?

Daddy — Stewart MacBride — however, said that God helped those who helped themselves, and that he and Mama were going to restore the Nettie-MacBride family names to their rightful place in mountain society. Make people stop whispering that they were cast-offs raised by kinfolk, both from histories rumored to be scandalous. Family was everything. Mama and Daddy's merged pride would bring a golden glow back to the MacBride name. They would open a restaurant, like Mama's cousin Delta Whittlespoon had done over at the Crossroads Cove, and it would be the best restaurant in Asheville.

Daddy couldn't cook, but he could be a redheaded Rock of Gibraltar. His first calling: Family. Taking care of Mama and us. Second? Taking care of the good citizens of

Asheville and his fellow police officers, just as he'd taken care of his brother soldiers in Vietnam. Third: Making our family so rich that we could hire people to whack people who stole from the front-yard smokers.

Family Family Family. Always Family. If you weren't some kind of Family to us, you weren't on the radar. Not in Daddy's world. Or mine.

Jay
Jay Becomes the Landlord

"Turn there, please," I said to Lawyer George.

He and his wife and their baby now shared the top floor of a 1910 piano manufacturing factory Dad had left me, just a block off the busy streets of Pack Square. Even after Dad renovated it, the high-ceiling, thick-beamed industrial loft was drafty and haunted; even when Dad was with me, it felt like we were floating on a forgotten cloud above the streets just one story below. I liked the feeling, still.

Lawyer George steered Dad's vintage diesel Mercedes out of town and down a steep hill into the old river district, where the shells of forgotten mills and factories moldered along the French Broad. Dad (and now I) owned three properties the city kept threatening to firebomb, but he had been talking to local artists about turning them into studios. Lawyer George had all of Dad's notes about that.

"Across the river?" Lawyer George said worriedly, as if we needed shots and a passport. He waved a hand against the summer wind. The Diesel Farter had no air conditioning. We puttered across the bridge above the French Broad and up the hill into the wilds of West Asheville. Kind of the 'burbs that time forgot. Some old brick store fronts lined the main drag that ran atop the ridge, forming a spine for steep, narrow streets that dropped down through thick forest and kudzu jungles. Most of the houses were little clapboard cottages from before the 1950s, and they weren't in good condition.

"Delta said this is where they live."

She said if I wanted to "do right," I could at least make friends with Jane Eve — Emma's daughter — and her family. Nobody would ever know if Arlo was Jane Eve's father; he had been in prison for attacking Great-Grandfather when Jane Eve was born. The dates were vague; there had been another man in Emma's life after Arlo went to prison. No one talked about the details, and Emma died when Jane Eve was just a few weeks old.

So Jane Eve MacBride — a Nettie on her mother's side — was probably not the Claptraddle heir, and I couldn't give her Free Wheeler anyway, if she was. I'd keep very quiet about all that history.

The less your uncle knows about the places and the people you love, the safer they'll be, Dad had always told me.

"I hope these people have electricity," Lawyer George said. "Plumbing. A roof. I should have asked my wife to pack my camping gear."

We turned off down a lane where wisteria and trumpet creeper vine hung over the pavement in purple/orange chaos. We rattled past fallen mailboxes and overgrown foundations, skirting the fingers of cracked driveways that disappeared into the roots of trees that owned them now, and rounded a curve into what, by then, seemed to me to be a wonderland of nothing.

That's when the sides of the lane opened up, having been bush-hogged enough to let cars park on the sides. A line of cars two dozen long filled both sides, stretching down the shady lane and around another curve. Pickups and old sedans, BMWs and junkers, minivans and Jaguars. Even a couple of small tour buses.

The hair rose on the back of my neck. *Must be a funeral.*

Lawyer George drove slowly, arrowing between the narrow space left in the middle. People strolled past, casually dressed, many carrying take-out boxes and containers. Beyond the bend, a huge oak tree shadowed a big new metal mailbox painted white with MACBRIDE on the side in fat red letters. Parked cars continued past the mailbox and down a wooded hill.

I gazed out my open window at an old cottage sporting fresh paint and lots of repairs, a sunny, mown lawn full of metal monsters I couldn't quite describe, and a big side yard — over an acre — filled with picnic tables shaded by a couple of big trees plus tents and umbrellas. Every table was full of people, and every person was busy eating mounds of food off mismatched china plates.

I pointed at an Asheville police car parked far down the lane. "Mr. MacBride is a police officer. It must be all right to park on the street. I'll take over from here. You go in and discuss the lease offer. I'll park the car."

After all, I tested at a learner's permit level of maturity according to my teachers at Horizon. The Horizon Academy was that alternative-ed school. I had a feeling Officer

36

MacBride wouldn't be impressed by tests that included a section on psychic awareness. But I was a Wakefield and accustomed to certain privileges. Lawyer George hemmed and hawed, then shrugged and gave in.

I was determined to be the master of my lonely fate and to honor Dad's devotion to doing good things for the people around him, the community, the less fortunate than us. Somehow, this web of the spirit would hold our islands together, would keep their foundations inside us.

Gabby

"Ralph!" Ralph said. Then the dog in our family tore off toward the front yard, barking *Ralph Ralph Ralph* in all his big-part-Shepherd glory, meaning that another thief was meddling with the herd of fifty-gallon drums Daddy had hillbilly-engineered into the delivery system for Mama's secret barbecue rubs and slow-cooking sauces. Two sides of beef, five slabs of pork ribs, an entire flock of chickens, and five deer haunches from last fall's hunting season were at stake. Not to mention my pickles.

"Stand down, Baby Sister, I'll go this time," Gus called. He liked to talk military-speak. Gus was already planning a career in the army, following in Daddy's footsteps. But for now, my ten-year-old brother was serving KP duty, up to his elbows in a ten-gallon pot of unmixed coleslaw. He had mayonnaise in his red eyebrows and pieces of red cabbage in his brown-red hair. The white apron over his t-shirt and jeans was smeared with red barbecue sauce. He looked like he'd murdered a Cabbage Patch Doll.

"I'm going," Tal said, and scurried away from her plastic table full of cookie dough Mama had given her to play with. She was an inventive five-year-old, and practiced recipes that were often wonderful but often . . . not. At the moment she was putting cabbage in the dough.

Gus jerked his hands out of the pot as she rushed past him. When he sank a freckled hand into her red braids, smearing mayonnaise and slaw on her forehead, she turned and stared up at him from beneath coleslaw bangs. He started laughing, and so did she.

Not me. I grabbed the longest, thickest metal spoon from the mixing set on my table. We were all on the back screened porch, where a pair of big floor fans kept Mama's outdoor prep area just this side of fly-free to avoid a health-department citation. The whole home-restaurant operation was scooting past the authorities on a wink and a nod because Daddy was a police officer — and because the mayor, the police chief, the fire chief and most of the city council were Mama's customers.

I left a tub of baked beans still in need of honey and a tub of mac 'n' cheese waiting for grated cheddar. Mama and Daddy were inside talking to a suit-wearing stranger carrying a clipboard and a stack of papers. I wouldn't interrupt them with another to-do in the yard; besides, I was a team player in a family business. I was good at being the family's hit woman.

The Boy was unlike any boy I'd ever seen before. I halted behind a big butterfly bush next to the house, watching him study the smokers while Ralph did a complete out-of-character transformation and licked his leg. Ralph had never seen a boy in our shabby West Asheville neighborhood wearing a white Polo shirt, tan chinos and fancy loafers. I certainly hadn't, either.

He was at least as tall as Gus, who often got mistaken for older than ten. He already had shoulders like a teenager, and long legs. His hair was black and a little shaggy. It didn't quite match the rest of them. But then, neither did the wide leather cuff he wore around one wrist. Some kind of charms dangled from it. Topping off his fascinating attire was a bright yellow Sports Walkman, hanging from his leather belt. The ear wires dangled from his pocket. Ralph licked them.

He had a Walkman. A Walkman! To die for.

Chocolate ice cream covered in Reese's Pieces. That's what he loves more than any other food in the world. But he won't ever eat it. Why?

My quirky talent was sensing a person's soul food — not just a favorite dish, but something that has special meaning. Gus got a sweet or sour sensation about people, and when he described it to Mama and Daddy, using words like "apple cider, lemonade, the smell of an old tennis shoe or maybe burned coffee," Daddy grinned and told him he was cut out to be a beer tester. Tal's foodie talent was a little hard to decipher so far, but Mama was betting on something to do with smells. For one thing, the first time baby Tal said "Mama" was when Mama was waving a spoonful of warm apple pie under Tal's nose.

The Boy turned to tuck his ear wires into his pocket. Under that shaggy black hair were serious dark eyes, a long sturdy nose like Ralph's, and a sad mouth that quirked at the edges when he scuffed a hand over Ralph's head.

My heartbeat was very attached to The Boy already. My spoon-wielding hand wavered by my bean-smeared apron. Bees buzzed around my knobby knees under the hems of cut-offs, and the hot July sun was making the freckles make baby freckles along the straps of my tank top. I ignored it all to gaze in hypnotized wonder at the sweet-deprived prince who had won Ralph's lickability award and my forgiveness for invading the smoker herd.

But then he turned back to the smoker in front of him, and opened the lid.

Not that one. If he'd meddled in any other smoke-puffing cooker, I'd have sauntered over calmly. But he opened the canister that included a big aluminum pan full of my personal specialty, my signature dish, the homemade dill pickles stuffed with bacon, minced hotdog, and sweet cheese.

At only eight, I was already the self-proclaimed Pickle Queen of West Asheville.

He reached into the smoker, plucked a Smoky Dill Oink from its bed, sniffed it, and nibbled one end. I held my breath. My Oinks were a big hit with Mama's customers.

His face scrunched as if he'd swallowed

pure vinegar. He spit the piece on the grass, then walked over to a hedge of honeysuckle and tossed the Smoky Dill Oink into its guilt-hiding tangle.

By then, I was heading for him with the spoon raised for attack.

Jay
Gabby Swings a Spoonful of Love at First Sight

Gabby left her mark on me. In my scalp, to be precise. A half-inch gash at the edge of my hairline. Draw a line ten degrees off plumb from the end of my right eyebrow to hairline, and there's the fine white scar to this day.

I bled like a razor-sliced street fighter, which didn't stop her from whacking me on the forearms as I gallantly shielded myself without running or fighting back. Ralph barked merrily. Gus ran around front to see if his sister was being attacked; he got a laugh out of that, later. I was a little unhappy about being cracked on the skull with a spoon, so when he shoved me away from Gabby and yelled at me as if I were to blame, I punched him in the shoulder. I was nobody's wimpy little orphaned rich kid. Unfortunately, Gus was trained in the fine art of My Old Man Is A Cop And I Can

Kick Your Ass, and so he tackled me.

We rolled around among the smokers, slugging and grunting, sharing my blood, while Gabby danced around us, hitting me with the spoon again at every opportunity. In the background I heard "Ka pow, ka pow," which I'd later learned was Tal, cheering us on.

Gnarly hands dug into my neck. Gus and I were dragged apart by a skeleton with dead blue eyes.

"What are you doing here?" the skeleton yelled at me. "Wakefield! Tom Wakefield's boy! He's dead and now you come creeping around! Why?" He snatched me by my shirt front. "Your uncle sent you. Admit it. It's a trap. Well I won't let you get them! You won't get your claws into this family!" He shook me hard.

"Mr. Sam!" Gus yelled.

I jerked angrily. "Let go of me, sir."

By now, Gus had a strong hold on Mr. Sam's arm, Tal was hiding in the honeysuckle by the side yard fence, and Gabby bounded forward, dropping her lethal spoon. She squirmed boldly beneath the old man's other arm, wrapping her arms around his and bracing herself against his leg like a chock block. "Come on, Mr. Sam," she said softly, "Get your mind back to today. Let go of him. He's just a pickle thief, that's all."

I scowled at her. "*Not* a thief. I planned to pay for it. I don't steal. Not anything from anybody."

"Food waster."

"I do not . . . it was only because . . ."

"He's a Wakefield!" the man yelled again. "Don't you understand? A Wakefield!"

"Hey, Mr. Sam, hey," Gus said, putting a raw-knuckled hand on his forearm. "Remember what Mama and Daddy said. Stay peaceful. Or they won't let you have your flask back."

"The Buddha," he drawled in a hoarse but elegant voice, as he reached out to thumb the charms that hung from my leather wrist cuff. He bent low, swaying like a scarecrow sagging off its pole in the wind. "And a crucifix, and a Star of David. Your Daddy was looking to protect and guide you in every way he could. Because he knew what it means to be a Wakefield!"

"He's gone crazy," Gabby whispered to her brother. "He's gone nut-pickled candy-corn bonkers, this time. *Mr. Sam.* Please. Please calm down."

A shiver went through me. It was as if the Grim Reaper had paid a visit to me — again. He had stark white hair and a dirty gray beard with bare patches around his pale lips. He wore a faded, double-breasted suit over a David Bowie t-shirt, a strand of love beads, and cheap metal necklace with a tarnished charm on it: an old-fashioned type of bicycle. On his feet were thick leather hiking sandals. He wore no socks, and he had painted his long, blunt toenails pink.

He stared down at me with those sunken eyes burning inside folds of skin mottled in veins and red splotches. Suddenly, he snatched my wrist in his bony grip.

"I'm not condemning your daddy. He's the only good Wakefield ever born, as best I can tell. It's up to you to be like him. Or be damned! I'll come back from my grave and haunt you forever if you stray down the path of Augustus! And so will he!"

Augustus? He'd known my great-grandfather?

"Let me go, sir," I repeated.

"Mr. Sam," Gus warned.

"Who are you?" I asked.

"Sam Osserman," the old skeleton said, yellowed teeth bared at me. "Why are you here? I guard this family! From Wakefields! Tell me why you've come here, boy! And who is that yellow-haired hired gun you sent inside?"

"His name's George Avery. He's here to offer Mr. and Mrs. MacBride a lease on a

45

building in town. Because I asked him to."

Gus and Gabby stared at me, then at each other, then at me again.

Mr. Sam's putrid eyes narrowed into a sinister squint. "Why'd you ask him to?"

"Because . . ."

Because Delta Whittlespoon was with me when Dad died, and now, every time I miss him so much I think I'll explode, I think of biscuits and remember her hug. Because she sends me biscuits every week in the mail. Because she told me that Mrs. MacBride's mother was a cousin of Mary Eve Nettie's.

Mary Eve Nettie is the reason Dad died knowing Free Wheeler would stay in one piece and that he'd beaten E.W for once. Mary Eve Nettie gave Dad a kind of peace. And she's why I can keep Free Wheeler away from E.W. Just like Dad wanted.

So I'm going to take care of her family. A family that loves and hugs and believes biscuits can heal the world. A family that's nothing like mine.

"Because I like biscuits," I said. "Because I'm rich, and I own buildings all around Asheville, and I want a diner around the corner from where I live, and I hear that Mrs. MacBride makes good biscuits."

"Liar!"

"No, it's true," Gabby put in. She was

watching me closely. "It's true. Mr. Sam. He's got biscuit witchery around him. Gus?"

Gus nodded. "Yep. Not sure how it got there, exactly, but it's there."

The old skeleton sneered. "He's hiding something."

"Come on, Mr. Sam," Gus soothed.

I looked up into those strange eyes, and that bicycle charm necklace, and said, "Did you know a bicycle man named Arlo Claptraddle?"

He froze. I could almost hear his bones rattle. Fear whitened his ashy skin even more. He began to shake. He released me and stumbled backward, shaking his head. "Oh, no, you won't fool me. You won't pull me into your web. You'll not get to my loved ones through your wily Wakefield ways. No no no."

Gus and Gabby looked embarrassed. "Sorry," she said. "He won't hurt us or anybody else. He lives in our garage. With his bikes."

"Don't tell him about my bicycles, child!" the old man shouted. Then he hunkered over and waved his hands at me. "You're the only hope for Wakefield redemption! Swear it! Swear on her soul! Swear!"

"Whose soul, sir?"

"Swear it," the old man roared. "Jayson

Wakefield, son of Thomas Anthony Wakefield, rest his soul, grandson of the worthless William Wakefield, great-grandson of Augustus Wakefield, damn his bloody soul! Swear you are not bred to sink into greed and lust and meanness and cruelty and the pride that stalks and betrays any and all who trust your bloodline. *Swear you will be the man your father wanted you to be!* Swear!"

Part of me just wanted to get his cold, dead stare off my brain, but something deeper provoked me to make a promise. "I swear," I said grimly. I had come here on the first of three long-term missions: to take care of Mary Eve Nettie's family, to protect Free Wheeler, and to destroy E.W. If I had to swear allegiance to causes I didn't understand, so be it.

Sam searched my eyes until I thought my head would melt. He swiveled toward Gus. "He'll need your friendship."

Gus cocked a scraped eyebrow. "Sure, Mr. Sam. You bet."

"Don't you joke with me, sir! Swear it!"

Gus frowned at me. "I don't even know him."

"Use your gift, Groucho MacBride!"

"Groucho?" I intoned.

Gus looked like he might slug me. He leaned toward me, tilting his head.

One time in New Orleans, a woman who worked for Dad's architectural consultants, knowing that Dad was friendly to the subjects of all things metaphysical, studied him and me with the same crow-watching-a-cricket stare. "What is it?" Dad said, encouraging her.

"My grandmother believed in African Voodoo. Me, no. But I see . . . spirits around some people. Your son is . . . accompanied. They follow him. He's a magnet. He's a key."

Dad had simply nodded. "A turning point, I hope."

"Smooth," Gus finally said. "No burn." He looked at Mr. Sam. "Clean. I swear. I'll be Jay Wakefield's friend."

Sam dragged Gabby from under his arm, but gently. She continued holding onto him, scowling from him to me to Gus. He pointed at her. "He'll need more than your friendship. He'll need your womanly love."

Her mouth fell open.

So did mine.

"Swear you'll love him!"

"Mr. Sam, I'm . . . I'm just a kid . . . and . . . he threw my Smoky Dill Oink away!"

"I don't eat pork," I said quickly. "I'm a vegetarian."

"I don't care what church you go to, you don't throw my stuffed pickles in the honey-suckle!"

Sam jabbed his finger at her. "Close your eyes, Greta Garbo MacBride! Tell me what your food angel thinks about him."

I gave her a look. She shot back, "You repeat that name and I'll whack you again."

"Truce."

"Concentrate!" Mr. Sam bellowed.

"I already know, Mr. Sam. Chocolate ice cream with Reese's Pieces! He loves that more than any food in the whole world. But he won't eat it because . . ." She looked at me, frowning harder. "Oh. Oh." Her face softened. Her red brows shifted.

"Private information?" Sam asked.

I stared at her in disbelief, but there was no doubt. She pinned it. My favorite. And I never let myself eat it; I'd taken a vow not to eat any sweets, because . . . Dad couldn't. *She knew.*

You just want to fit in. You want a family.

The thought came out of nowhere and hit me in the chest. No. I was here to take care of business.

"You think a lot," Gus said. He snorted. "I see smoke coming out of your ears."

I snorted back. "I don't see anything coming out of yours."

We shoved each other, but it was half-hearted. Gabby hissed at us. "Boys!" She went over to the smoker, opened the lid, reached into the pan of Smokey Dill Oinks, retrieved one and set it delicately on the palm of her hand, though her hand was covered in bits of grass from scuffing around on the lawn while hitting me with the spoon. She prodded the innards, flicking all the meat out of the pickle. Ralph caught most of the bits in mid-air and vacuumed the rest. Gabby carried the de-Oinked Smoky Dill to me and held it out. A peace offering. "Pickles. Your new favorite food."

I had blood all over my face, some dirt in the back of my mouth, and felt not only the freaky mysterious ray of Sam Osserman's gaze on me but also Gus's head-cocked scrutiny, since the old man was sort of marrying his sister to me.

Somewhere in the honeysuckle bushes, Tal said, "Pineapple. Pine and apple. Piney apple. That's his smell. Good good good. Appley pine. I swear to be his friend, too! I swear, too. Hey. A snake."

Which sent Gus hurrying over to check it out.

I took the warm pickle from Gabby and made sure I didn't hesitate. I shoved the whole thing in my bloody, dirty mouth, chewed hard, and swallowed in three big gulps. The actual taste was lost on me. But the soul taste was fine.

What I really remember was the way Gabby watched me, with worried green eyes in a face spattered with freckles the color of ginger. A mass of cinnamon-red hair spilled around her shoulders and arms in poofy braids. I wasn't sure if the orangey smears on her girl-sized chef's apron were food or the blood of some animal she'd brained with the spoon.

My world was an island up in the loft of a building where I lived with people I liked and respected but who were not my family and who, though very trusted, were paid well to stay there. I had only ever had one true emotional connection to another person — the pure jolt of love that came from Dad. That was the only time I'd felt I mattered much to any other person on the planet. Until now. Gabby MacBride lasered a lightning bolt of belonging into me that lit up all sorts of untested circuits. It wasn't romantic, or sexual, not for a long time to come.

At any moment she might pulp me with a kitchen utensil. But the mere fact that something made her care — that something she saw in me was so special she offered me her sacred smoked pickle without the holy Oink — made me happy in ways I couldn't describe.

"I swear," she said to Sam.

Gabby

Even in the high mountains of western North Carolina, the rain can scare people. That's why Asheville was built at the top of a ridge over the Swannanoa and French Broad Rivers, safe above the floods. Down in the lowlands, those waters killed people; there were flood marks twenty feet high on the aged sides of the river buildings, even at the fancy English-cottage-style village outside the Vanderbilts' estate, where the workers had lived at the turn of the century. But high up on the humpback of the Asheville peak, we were dry and happy in the echoing emptiness of our dream come true, the brick-over-granite two-story shop building that had been built in 1910 by Benjamin Ackman Wakefield, elder brother of Augustus, using granite mined in Wakefield quarries and bricks made in Wakefield kilns. The entrance walkway said P, B, and S in black-and-white ceramic tile, for the original owners — Parner, Brewster, and Sons Leather Goods.

We were surrounded by tools, saws, sawdust, lumber and plans, as a river of water sluiced down Lexington's old gray pavement and cracked sidewalks. Thunder rumbled and lightning cracked.

Me, Gus, Tal, Mama and Daddy ate a feast from plastic bowls set out on a folding table covered in a celebration table cloth — old linen embroidered with roses — that Mr. Sam had given Mama. Where he got such a fine thing, and what the roses meant, no one knew.

"He was mean to Jay," Tal said.

"You know why?" Daddy said that day, as we sat around on the floor of our dream come true. "Because something got hold of his heart, something hateful, and he won't let it go. People who won't let go are ruined."

Mama peered at him, a half-smile on her mouth. "You sure you're from around these parts? Scots-Irish? Feuds aren't feuds until they're two generations old."

"That's just the point, Jane. It's crazy to have hates and feuds and wars that drag on. Heartbreaks and even misunderstandings. It's a rot. If I were a Bible thumper, I'd call it a sin."

"Is that why we're doing business with a Wakefield?" Gus asked.

Daddy's rusty-brown brows flattened. He

gave us his Sarge MacBride chin tilt. We stopped eating and straightened to attention. "Listen up," he said.

"Stewart, wait." Mama got up and said to Tal, "Come on, Biscuit Witch, you've got cupcake icing all over you. Let's go try out the plumbing."

"But I wanta listen up," Tal said.

Mama led her out of the main room. Ralph got up to follow, then yawned and flopped back down.

Daddy leaned toward Gus and me intently. "Tom Wakefield was a good man. Loved. I guess I got nothing against mining as a business, if it's done right, but the Wakefields sure don't let fairness or common decency stand in the way of getting rich. Tom saw a bigger picture than just making money."

I said quietly, "I saw a history book at the library. It says there was a moonshine war between MacBrides and Wakefields."

"There's gossip. Going back to moonshiner days, yep. There were a lot of Mac-Brides up in the high mountains then, the Little Finn Valley. They farmed, and they mined, too. Mostly mica, but some quartz. There was a war during moonshining times. They fought the law, and the law won. Wiped them out. The Wakefields got hold of the valley. Mined what they could find, decided it wasn't worth it. Sold out to their cousins from Louisiana. Bonavendiers. Kind of a luckless bunch, those Cajuns. Been there ever since. Tom Wakefield was friendly with them, I hear." He shook his head. "I don't think those MacBrides were our people."

"What if they were?" Gus asked quietly. "What if Wakefields killed a bunch of our family?"

"I killed Vietnamese men back in the early seventies, but I don't hold any grudges now. And I lost friends to those Vietnamese soldiers. Times change. You let go. Those who won't let go of old prejudice, they don't see straight. They turn out like Mr. Sam." Daddy sat back on his lean butt, which was cased in dusty painters' pants, and slapped his knees. "Enough such talk. We got work to do." He thumbed toward Mama's proud outdoor sign, which had just been delivered that morning. It stood against one wall: The P, B and S Diner.

Pickled, Baked and Stewed. Mama and Daddy named the diner for me, Tal and Gus. "Stewed" for Gus because they couldn't come up with a better word for his cooking talent. "He's goin' to be a beer man," Daddy announced. "He knows his brew. His stew."

"Ralph," Ralph said, rolling around and wagging. We pivoted toward the shop's heavy glass door between wide bay windows, where Mama planned to put tables with flower boxes on them.

Jay Wakefield stood there with the rain slogging down on him, one fist raised to knock on the glass.

I shoved my sandwich into a napkin and ran to let him in. A whoosh of soggy air and wet wind whirled rain, thunder and even a flash of lightning around him, as if the storm was spitting him at us. His black hair clung to his face. He shivered inside faded jeans and a white t-shirt and jeans. Even the laces on his jogging shoes shook. The talismans on his wrist cuff jingled.

Mama came rushing out of the back. "Get those clean paint rags out of the storage room," Mama told Daddy. "Let's dry this boy off before he catches cold."

"I c-came to work." His teeth chattered.

"As what, a mop?" I said.

His mouth flattened.

Mama said, "Greta Garbo MacBride, a word, please, ma'am."

Shit.

I followed her into a back room where our newly-leased kitchen equipment sat in the middle of the floor like cows that had gotten loose from a pasture. Daddy's buddies from the police department were coming over that night to wire the walls for a commercial stove, ovens, and a cooler.

Mama pulled me around a corner that led to a back door alley. "Jay lost his daddy no more than six weeks ago. His mama abandoned him and his daddy when he was a baby. He's an orphan. And you, my sour pickle, are a mean little thing sometimes."

I winced. "I just . . . I don't know how to talk to him. Why'd his mama leave?"

"Because she was a prissy rich girl, and she married to get richer. She decided being married to a Wakefield with sugar diabetes was no fun — not to mention Tom Wakefield wasn't interested in parties and mansions and buying yachts. So she went off to Europe and married a Spaniard."

"Good riddance."

Mama rubbed her forehead, releasing poofs of reddish-brown hair that, to me, symbolized her lack of pretense. She never "put on airs." Tal said Mama's essence was apple pie — pretty obvious, but I agreed — yet to me, Mama was a sweet gherkin, my favorite pickle. "That boy out there —" she nodded toward Jay's direction — "held his daddy's hand while he died. Cousin Delta said it broke her heart to watch how the life drained out of both of them at the same time, just in different ways."

"So Jay's gonna live with that Lawyer George from now on?"

"Yes. It's a bad situation. His daddy and uncle were at odds. So he's got no family. Except us now, if he'll have us. Lord knows he needs us."

"I'll be nicer. But . . . he makes me feel funny."

"Then just keep quiet."

That was going to be a problem.

I went back out front. He put a hand to his heart, dripping water on the bare wood floor, forming a wide puddle. "If you don't want a Wakefield around, just say so. I understand."

Gus rolled his eyes. "I can handle any trouble a Wakefield dishes out."

Daddy started fixing a plate. "Do Wakefields eat regular food so long as there's no meat in it?"

"Yes, sir."

"Okay, then."

I said loudly, "You're dripping on the *floor*," and stomped over to scrub him with a roll of paper towels I grabbed off the folding table. "And we have work to do. Because once we get done here, Mama says we're going to a movie, and you better be dried off because you'll stink like Ralph after he rolls in a puddle, and I'm not sharing my popcorn with you at the movie if you *stink,* ugggh." As I scoured his hair, barely missing the gash on his forehead where two stitches sealed the wound from my serving spoon, he looked down at me as if I was crazy plus funny and somehow all right. Maybe his eyes were wet with rain or maybe not.

Either way, I mashed them with the paper towels.

He smiled.

Over the next year, the P, B and S Diner made so much money that Mama and Daddy were able to stop just renting the house in West Asheville and put a down payment on it. We stopped using the side yard as a restaurant — one step ahead of the county health department, even though the inspector was a customer and said he'd never seen a cleaner back-porch kitchen. Daddy moved the smokers to an alley beside the P, B and S and put in high chain gates on both ends, so they'd be safe at night. The aroma they gave off drew people from all over that part of the city. When street people came by, we still offered the

Eat now, Pay later, plan.

Mama and Daddy paid off the loan they'd taken to set up the kitchen and furnishings. Pretty soon Mama was getting written up in everything from the *Asheville Citizen-Times* to the *Atlanta Journal-Constitution* and *Southern Living.* Cousin Delta came over the Crossroads and the two of them posed for pictures that went all the way to *Newsweek* magazine under the headline: *The Biscuit Witches of North Carolina Bring Their Kitchen Charms to Appalachian Cuisine On The Cusp of a New Millennium.*

The work was constant — for Mama every day, with Tal as her dough-happy mascot; for me and Gus after school and on weekends, for Daddy in all his hours outside his duty shifts, and for Jay, who became our new brother. He was there every day as well, dropped off by Lawyer George after "school" at the strange place he attended, and on weekends.

The only dark moments involved Jay's uncle. There were times when Lawyer George dropped in unexpectedly, looking grim, and then he and Jay would go into the diner's little office and close the door. Even though Jay was too young to sign contracts and Lawyer George had been left in charge of all his business decisions,

Lawyer George was training him, consulting, just as he'd promised Jay's dad that he'd do. Jay would come out of those meetings looking angry, and he wouldn't talk to me about any of it. He wouldn't share anything with anyone. Daddy bought two pairs of boxing gloves and hung a boxing dummy in the back hall. Gus was put in charge of challenging Jay to boxing matches when he got that Look on his face. That helped.

Other than those incidents, the years he spent with us were happy. We almost forgot that when he turned eighteen Jay would inherit millions, then more millions at twenty-one, and at twenty-five, several tens of millions, plus so many buildings and pieces of land that Lawyer George began teaching him how to use an amazing portable computer that he toted around, only the size of a big briefcase, to keep track of it all.

One day, Jay would outgrow us. I tried not to think about that.

I turned ten and decided it was time I kissed him.

Jay

Gabby Likes the Thrill of the Chase

On her birthday, she locked me in the diner's cooler because I refused to let her kiss me. I was twelve, she was ten. I'd spent months trying to ignore her eye batting; to dodge her, humor her, and most of all, not do anything that would make Gus, my best buddy, challenge me to a fist fight. But she was a redheaded piranha with lips.

"Knock three times when you change your mind," she said.

Finally, my teeth chattering, I gave up and knocked.

When she opened the door I said, "I l-lied," and stumbled past her.

"Not fair!" she squealed. She slugged me in the chest. I was so stiff from the cold that I tripped over a crate of turnips and hit the floor hard. When I just lay there for a few seconds, blinking slowly, she bent over me, her big green eyes worried. "Jay? Jay!"

I sat up, holding the side of my head and squinting at her. "I'm fine. Go knock down someone your own size." Pretty witty, since I was a foot taller.

Her face relaxed, the freckles riding a big, relieved smile. "But that's too easy. You're more fun." She delivered the coup de Gabs by lunging forward and kissing me on the mouth — a soft, damp, smush of a kiss, untrained, unasked for, and unappreciated. And yet, I've never forgotten it.

"Got you," she said softly. "Forever."

She bolted out of the kitchen, leaving me to make up some damn good excuse for the knot on my head so Gus would never find out that his little sister had suckered me into a trap, knocked me on my ass, and kissed me against my will.

Looking back on that moment, I knew it was Forever, too.

Jay
January 1991, the End of Our Childhood
I admit I didn't enjoy serving people the way Gabby, Gus and Tal did. I wasn't a good "front" worker, as Mama MacBride put it. Yes, I called her that. I called Mr. MacBride "Sarge." He liked it. He understood why I couldn't honor him with Dad's title. Anyhow, one-on-one with a customer, I didn't like being treated like a servant. One time I heard a police officer buddy of Sarge's mimic Yoda and say, "Strong the Wakefield is in that one, yes," and everyone guffawed. Gabby came over and punched me on the arm in a show of support.

But on Saturdays it was fun to sell biscuits, cookies and, of course, homemade pickles on the streets, something Gus, Gabs and I did every weekend if the weather was good. We roamed the sidewalks around Pack Square, Pritchard Park, Haywood Street and the Flatiron Building with shallow baskets strapped around our necks. Business was good and we got to keep twenty cents on every sale.

I was more proud of my income as a street vendor than of all the trust fund money that existed in bank accounts I'd only inherited. *We didn't earn the fortune we've been given,* Dad always said. *It's only ours to manage until we pass it along to the next generation. We have to prove we deserve the responsibility.*

But my street money was honest cash, mine alone, and I stored it in my bedroom at the loft, dropping each Saturday's coins into an empty gallon coffee can I'd saved from the diner's trash and washed. My money. My bank.

My family.

"Hotahotahotahota biscuits!" Gus sang out at the corner of College and Haywood. "Sausage and cheese, or only buttered if you please, fresh made, homemade, The P, B and S Diner, nothing finer!"

And on the other corner Gabby bellowed, "Pickles on a stick, fat, fresh and thick, spicy or sweet, a homemade treat! Eat 'em real quick! Stick 'em in your mouth! Make 'em head south!"

I, who simply stood across the street saying, "Hot food for sale," in a low voice, stared across at Gus. We traded a strangled look. Gabs invented new chants all the time, but this one . . .

Gus clamped a hand to his forehead. People were scowling at her. Or laughing. She looked bewildered and a little annoyed. I crossed the street as soon as the light changed. She shook her head at me. "What?"

"Uhmmm, go back to last week's holler."

"Why?"

"Because otherwise Gus will come over here and explain why, and you won't like it."

"Why don't *you* just explain?"

"Just go back to last week's sales pitch."

Her eyes narrowed. The slightest crinkle at the corner of her right eye alerted me that I'd been had. "Because it sounds like I'm talking about penises?"

An older lady halted. "What are you doing out here begging for money on the street and talking like that? Does your mother know you're here?"

"She sent me," Gabby said solemnly. "We

need money for an operation to save his leg." She pointed at me. "He was bitten by a tarantula."

I was speechless. The woman looked down at the jeans extending from under my quilted jacket. "Where?"

"I . . . no . . . ma'am . . ."

"On his penis," Gabby said. "But the poison spread."

She drew up like a mad hen. "Where are your parents?"

"The tarantulas got them already."

I groaned. Steadying my basket with one hand, I grabbed Gabs by the sleeve of her long denim coat. "We're going now. I'm sorry, ma'am. She's . . . she didn't take her pills this morning. We have to go."

"Oh, no, you're not," the woman ordered. "Just hold on. I'm getting to the bottom of this. Children on the street, in the cold, peddling food that's probably not safe to eat —"

"Hey, you take that back!" Gabs yelled. "These pickles are made by me! And these biscuits and cookies are made by Jane Eve Nettie MacBride, the best cook in Asheville. And if I want to stand on a street corner saying penis and telling people Jay Wakefield got bit on the penis by a tarantula —"

I wrapped an arm around her waist and

picked her up. She squealed. From the corner of my eye I saw Gus trotting towards us through a crowd on the crosswalk. I would bodily tote his sister to him, hand her over, and retreat to the piano factory until the memory of her joke faded from the hot red skin on my face.

She was already chortling. "If you won't have fun selling food then I have to show you how it's done," she told me over her shoulder. "So either get a chant or I'll keep making up ones you don't like!"

Gus reached us and suddenly he was looking past us with an expression on his freckled face that stopped me in my tracks and froze Gabs's laughter. She squirmed out of my grip. We turned to watch an Asheville police cruiser roar up to us, nearly bumping the sidewalk.

Charlie Bowman, Sarge's best friend, had tears on his beefy face. "Y'all need to get in," he said.

Gabby
Jay's Uncle Has Been Waiting . . .
Daddy was patrolling the roads outside downtown that morning. He'd just finished working a fender bender when a tractor-trailer slid on a patch of ice and sideswiped him. He died in the ambulance.

After his funeral, our little house was full of police officers. Delta commandeered the kitchen, since Mama sat on the living room couch with a thousand-mile stare in her eyes, with Tal curled up on her lap and Mr. Sam sitting beside them. Gus had gone down in the basement, where he and Ralph sat in the cold light of Daddy's propane hunting lantern. Daddy had had a funny little hobby. Knitting. Said it was something his own daddy had done for relaxation. He'd taught all three of us, but only Gus took to it. So Gus was in the basement, his back pressed to its raw clay wall, with Ralph's muzzle on his crossed legs, as he fumbled over the stitches of a gray wool scarf Daddy would never finish.

I stood on a high limb of the oak tree in the back yard, coatless in the freezing air, naked branches grabbing my trouser legs and pullover sweater. I looked down at the gray-brown yard twenty feet below, wondering how it would feel to hit it head first.

Wondering what Daddy felt when the tractor-trailer slammed into him.

Jay stepped into the center of my target spot, looking up at me with his dark, sad eyes. "You've always told me his food angel likes cornbread. I smell cornbread in the air. Don't you?"

I shook my head. Couldn't talk. My throat was full.

He talked for me. Told me that his daddy died at a place called Free Wheeler, near the Crossroads Cove, and that Cousin Delta was there, and how she not only smelled like biscuits she made Jay think of biscuits, warm and comforted. A memory that soothed him, later.

I didn't ask what he and his daddy had been doing way up there in the mountains or what kind of place Free Wheeler was. I just climbed down and went to him, crying without a sound. "Cornbread," I finally said.

He gave me a big hug and we stood there, me crying, him hugging. Slowly but surely, Daddy's food angel filled us with the rich spirit of Daddy's approval.

Jay

Everything was going wrong. Mama Mac-Bride put on a brave face but her cooking magic was gone. She couldn't remember recipes, couldn't concentrate when orders flooded through the window between the dining room and the kitchen. Gabby and Gus wanted to stay home from school to help, but she refused. The waitresses tried to cook but they didn't have the touch. Tal sat in her second-grade class not speaking

70

to anyone and drawing stick pictures of Sarge holding cookies. Delta took over the restaurant for three weeks while Mama MacBride found something to take her mind off her growing fear that she would never be able to make a living for her family again. Lawyer George and I came up with a plan: he had the authority to hire people. Fine, then. Mama MacBride would be my personal cook. And she could cook whenever she felt like it. Or not at all.

She turned the job down. I felt gobsmacked. Gabs grabbed me and gave me a sweet little kiss on one eyebrow, then she and Gus looked at me as if I were living on a different planet. "MacBrides don't take handouts," Gus said.

Case closed.

So in the end, it was decided to shut the doors of the P, B and S for "just a month or two." Mama MacBride took a job on the line at a small company that made potato chips, pork rinds and cheese crackers. She put on a hairnet and jumpsuit; she came home at night with cheese powder caked on her jogging shoes and the smell of old grease on her clothes.

I had all sorts of money but I couldn't help. It was like watching diabetes slowly destroy Dad.

And then E.W. made his move.

"L.G.?" I called out, listening to my voice echo a little among the tall ceilings of the piano factory. The huge loft had become home; the giant factory windows looking out over the city, the warren of big rooms divided by walls of thick vintage woods.

When I got home from school every afternoon, Lawyer George was usually at his desk in the area that served as offices. I knocked on the door of the apartment he shared with his wife, Vickie, and their baby son, Morrow, and was surprised when there wasn't an answer.

"I arranged for us to have a private moment," Uncle E.W. said, behind me.

I whirled to find him standing in the center of the main room, at ease among the walls filled with Dad's bookcases, commanding the islands of comfortable couches and tables stacked with more books. He was fifty years old then, with a slash of gray among the black hair at each temple; a big, hearty man with football shoulders. He wore fine suits; a soft dark gray one this time, with no tie and an open-collared shirt, as if he were ever casual about his appetites. He had four ex-wives and two daughters. Daughters didn't matter to him because they would marry and drop the Wakefield name. The one failing of his life was his inability to breed sons.

I was his only male heir. My curse.

"Hard times have befallen your MacBride friends," Uncle E.W. said.

Watch. Listen. Don't say too much. Lawyer George and I had spent a lot of time talking about ways to handle my uncle.

"They're doing okay."

"I understand you've tried to help them. I admire your maturity, Jay. It's hard to believe you're only twelve years old. I'll be honest with you. I wish you were my son."

I wanted to hit him. No, I wanted to kill him. The way he killed Dad.

"What do you want, sir?"

He sat down on the edge of a library table, drawing up one long leg, letting his polished shoe swing gently as he rested his hands on his knee. "I'm here to tell you that I'm going to have to step in."

My blood froze. "What do you mean, sir?"

"I'm really sorry, son . . ."

"I'm not your son."

The air chilled. His eyes, gray eyes like mine and Dad's, some called them wolf eyes, went dark. "I know you're fond of George Avery, and your dad trusted him, but it's come to my attention that he's been hiring people to spy on my business and steal information."

I could barely breathe. *I'll do whatever it takes to protect you,* Lawyer George had told me, more than once. *Your interests, not your uncle's. My job is to do what your Dad trusted me to do. And the one thing you and I both have to remember: Never trust your uncle.*

"Anything he did, I told him to do. I ordered him to do it."

"I see. Share some examples with me." My silence made him sigh. "That's honorable, Jay — your lie. Unfortunately, poor George is neither a very good attorney nor a very good corporate spymaster. I suspect the only reason your dad hired him was pity. As usual, he had a soft heart for a lapdog. George has made a very good friend for you, I do understand that. But he's not cut out to remain as your guardian, or as the manager of the estate you'll inherit when you're of age. Nine years from now. Your dad had a lot of faith in you. Most fathers wouldn't allow such a valuable estate to be turned over to their only child that early. But until then . . ."

I lunged forward, fists clenched. "I decide, not you! I want George back. And Vickie, and their baby. You leave George alone!"

"I can't do that. He's crossed some lines, and I have proof enough to force a change in your guardianship. What kind of uncle would I be if I let your legacy — which is part of the same legacy I share, and that my daughters share, the entire Wakefield legacy, no matter which of us controls what piece of it here and there — what kind of responsible steward of that legacy, of your future, would I be, if I didn't step in and take charge?"

"What'll happen to George?"

"That depends on you. I want you to give me a chance. Come be part of my world. Learn what I do, why I do it. I'd love to see you become my second-in-command someday. I'm not so bad. And if you give me a chance, I can be generous. George will lose his law license for what he's done. To my way of thinking, he deserves at least that, but he won't go to prison if you and I can come to an agreement. And your friends, we should talk about them. As your guardian, I have the authority to use your dad's money to help your friends as I see fit. And all I ask is that one day, when your dad's will turns control of the Free Wheeler property rights over to you is that you give me permission to mine it. You see, the fact that Mrs. Whittlespoon 'owns' the access

75

right doesn't mean she's the only one who has say-so. You'll be the property owner."

I shook my head. "I won't do it. Ever. Dad died there."

"I want you to grow up to be your own man, Jay. I had to learn that lesson, too. Your Grandfather William wasn't much of a role model. He drank, he gambled — obviously — he didn't manage the business very well. I had to grow up in a hurry. Your father was never healthy enough, or . . . strong-willed enough . . . to save our legacy, so I took over for the both of us. It wasn't fun. Or easy. Believe it or not, I was once an idealistic young boy like you. Let me help you face the realities."

He held out a hand. "Shake my hand. Give me your word that when you turn twenty-one you'll allow me to mine that property. In return, you'll get George back, and your MacBride friends will have all sorts of good luck. Wouldn't you like to see them make so much money they can afford to move into the city, open more restaurants, and live the kind of life we live?"

MacBrides don't take hand-outs.

Never trust your uncle.

"Can I think about it?"

He smiled just a little as his eyes went darker. "Jay, I am going to control your life for a long time to come. Anything that's not specifically spelled out or forbidden in your dad's will, I can handle as I see fit. Property management, rental rates, your education, where you live."

"He told Lawyer George how to handle all those things."

"That's not the same as putting them in a will. You can make your peace with that, or you can fight me. I hope to win you over."

My heart sank. No one was going to win anything. This was how it felt to fall on your own sword. To honor your father, to honor a promise you barely understood, but knew you had to honor it anyway. *I wouldn't destroy Free Wheeler, not for George's sake, not Mama MacBride's, Tal's, Gus's, not even Gab's. And certainly not for my own. I can't.*

"I'm never going to change what Dad wanted done. You can't make me. You won't hurt George. You won't hurt the MacBrides. I'll tell everyone who'll listen. I'll tell Sergeant Charlie. It's against the law to threaten people."

"We'll see," he said. And smiled.

Gabby

The P, B and S was going to re-open. Mama had come out of her misery enough to gather cleaning supplies, tie a bandana around her hair, and shoo the three of us into Daddy's pickup truck in our work clothes and with hopeful thoughts. It was a Saturday morning in March, with bright blue skies and the first warm pop of spring in the mountain air.

I tried to call Jay, but he didn't answer. I hadn't seen him since Thursday, which alarmed me. Since the diner closed in January, we'd stopped coming into town, but Lawyer George dropped him off at our house most days, to hang out.

"We'll walk up to Pack Square and rassle him out," Gus assured me. "Make him come get dusty and sweaty and mop some floors."

"I'll make him some cookies," Tal announced. She still wasn't talking much since Daddy died. Jay was a good influence.

Even Mama smiled, though the skin under her eyes was dusky blue, and when her mouth caught the light in an odd way it seemed to have a gray shadow around the lips. I hadn't gotten a sweet gherkin love-feel from her spirit since Daddy died.

But I felt almost cheerful. The streets were busy, the tourists were out, the guitar players and mimes and jugglers were warming up on the corners, and I began to hope we'd get back to our baskets full of biscuits, me and Gus and Jay, pushing the memory of January away, even as the spring sunshine made my eyes burn and tear.

We rattled down Lexington, just like the old days except for the giant empty spot where Daddy would never return. I was rubbing my eyes when Gus sank a hand onto my forearm so hard I yelled. Mama slammed the brakes. I threw one arm across Tal. Even wearing seatbelts, we almost hit the truck's dash.

Mama threw open her door and leapt out, almost getting hit by a car. Horns blared. She left the door hanging and ran toward the diner. Gus was already out of the truck and running after her, yelling at me to hold onto Tal. I snatched off our belts and hoisted Tal in my arms, struggling to climb out while craning my head around Tal's to see what Mama was staring at on the diner's door.

As I lumbered up behind her and Gus, the absolute shock nearly buckled my knees. The door was padlocked. An ugly yellow sign had been taped over the glass at eye level.

EVICTION NOTICE
Missed Payment - March
TW Properties

It couldn't be. TW Properties. Thomas Wakefield. Jay and Lawyer George. No way would Jay and Lawyer George throw us out of the diner just because Mama was late on one month's rent. Or ever late. Or not paying at all. Jay wouldn't. He *wouldn't.*

I whirled and headed up the sidewalk. "I'm going to find Jay!"

Mama put a hand to her chest and staggered. Gus grabbed her by one arm. Tal screamed. "Stand down, Gabby!" he yelled.

I took one look at Mama's face then hurried to the truck and helped him hoist her into the passenger side. Tal crawled in next, with me following. We held Mama upright while Gus drove to the emergency room.

"I'm just fine," Mama said that night, standing in our kitchen at home. She didn't look fine, and she wasn't fine, and we knew it. The ER doctor said her blood pressure was high, and had given her pills to take, plus something to calm her nerves. Now all we could do was pretend that everything would turn out okay if we helped her bake an apple pie. Tal stood beside her, holding a spoon in one hand and Mama's elbow by the other.

"Jay?" I said into the phone for the tenth time. I was talking to an answering machine with Lawyer George's voice on it. Again.

As I put the phone on its cradle in the living room, Gus and I traded a grim look. I shook my head. Tears burned my eyes. "He wouldn't 'go Wakefield' on us. No way."

Gus's mouth flattened. "I don't understand how Mama got kicked out of her lease, then."

From the kitchen came the sounds of the heavy glass pie dish hitting the linoleum and the soft thump as Mama slid to the floor with Tal desperately hanging onto her.

"Your Mommy had something wrong inside her head," the counselor said to us that night, at the hospital. "A kind of bubble. A little balloon." We sat on a couch in a small room where they take children to talk down to them — in well-intentioned ways. It had the dull psychic aroma of old bread, despite the low lights and soothing blue-gray walls and couch cushions sprayed to smell like comfort.

She's dead. Gus and I knew that. Mama had been dead when we held her cold hands. Dead when the doctors blocked our view of the monitors. We all felt her food spirit hug us, drift around us, drift into the part of us where, if we stayed very still and quiet, we could commune with her. Daddy was there, too, both of them. Which was why

Tal was curled up under the couch, not making a sound. Tasting them.

And then. "I smell liver," Gus said under his breath.

I nodded.

A very bad omen. From under the couch Tal said, "Chicken liver. We need to go."

Gus and I stood. The counselor, a small brown woman with big hair piled above little glasses, got up swiftly, flicking the clip of her ink pen while looking at us the way people do when three children spout strange non sequiturs after being told Mommy died of a brain aneurysm.

I knew how to massage a customer. "Would you mind if we took our baby sister around the corner to look out the big picture window at the mountains and the stars? The 'liver' thing is kind of our secret code for just needing to give each other a hug."

"Oh! Of course!" Looking relieved, she escorted us out the door and down the hall. "Right around there. Come on back whenever you're ready. I'll be here!"

The moment we were alone, we huddled in front of nighttime Asheville, that big lonely mountain sky over the city, all that beautiful emptiness out there beyond the thin glass. *Jay, where are you? What have*

82

you done? We held hands tightly, with Tal between Gus and me. "Why haven't they let us call anybody?" he said between gritted teeth. "I don't like the feel of this. We're leaving. And we're not asking anyone's permission."

"We'll go down those stairs," I agreed, looking at an emergency exit sign.

"Yeah. Once we get to the street I'll find the nearest cop. He'll call Charlie. Charlie'll come get us. And he'll call Delta. She'll take us to the Cove."

Tal tugged on our hands. "We have to go get Ralph and Mr. Sam, too."

"We will," Gus said.

"And then we'll have time to cry some more?"

We hugged her. We'd spend the rest of our lives crying, or trying not to.

Jay

I had been on lockdown in the loft for two days. The first sign that Lawyer George could not be kept away from me came when I heard tapping on the ceiling tile above my bed. As Dad's able-bodied assistant, he'd crawled through every nook and cranny of every building Dad owned, loving the old places as much as Dad did. His knowledge of the piano factory's rafters came in handy

83

when he lowered a knotted rope through an open ceiling tile in my bedroom. Uncle E.W. had stationed security people at the doors. To say Lawyer George was furious about the MacBrides' eviction was an understatement.

I climbed into the rafters, dressed for mountaineering, with a backpack full of Dad's books and my pockets heavy with change I'd earned selling biscuits. I had no immediate plan other than escaping, then telling Gabs, Gus, Tal and Mama MacBride about my new circumstances, then deciding what to do next, on Lawyer George's advice.

"How are you?" he whispered. "Here. My wife sent cookies."

In the beam of a flashlight his face looked sad and a little funny cased in a dark sock cap. He was only in his late twenties, and baby-faced. Lawyer George didn't fit the image of a burglar any more than he made a very good corporate spymaster. He had been doing what he felt he should to find out what Uncle E.W. planned, and he'd never told me he was doing anything underhanded. He protected me by just sharing what Thomas Wakefield's orphaned son needed to know: that my uncle was maneuvering to get control.

Lawyer George and I didn't speak again

until we were outside in the spring chill, at the bottom of a fire escape in the building's narrow alley. That's when Lawyer George took me by the shoulders and looked down at me sadly. "There's no easy way to tell you. This morning, Mrs. MacBride went to the diner and found an eviction sign on the door. Earlier tonight, at her home, she collapsed. She had a stroke. She's . . . she's dead."

I stumbled backwards and hit the wall. I wanted to yell and punch something. *Mama MacBride.* "Where are Gabs and Gus and Tal?"

They're at the hospital. We have to go get them. I have a bad feeling E.W. is closing in."

"Why would he . . . they don't mean anything . . . *he killed Mama MacBride.*" The horror struck me. *Because of me.* I stared at Lawyer George, who held onto my shoulders hard and looked worried.

"Jay? Jay? Talk to me."

I rasped out the details of my conversation with E.W. The deal he'd tried to strike. My refusal. *You can't make me.* "It's all my fault," I groaned. "He's taking revenge on them to punish me."

Lawyer George cupped my head as if that remark made him feel both sad and proud for me. "Let's go get your friends. My car's parked on a back street over —"

Headlights swung into the alley.

A big town car purred down the narrow lane. At the alley's other end, headlights blocked our retreat.

Uncle E.W.'s driver could be seen in the front seat.

Gabby

"Run!" Mr. Sam shouted. "I'll draw the monsters this way." He headed into the ER parking lot, flapping his bony arms and waving at the strangers trying to catch him, and us. Gus signaled me from behind a greening azalea hedge, using hand signals Daddy had taught us from his army days. I grabbed Tal's hand and shot down a shallow bank in the deep shadows behind a line of landscape lights. I heard Gus's footsteps heading up a gravel drainage lane.

If we can just find a regular policeman, one of Dad's buddies . . . why are we being chased instead of helped?

Tal stumbled and fell. I helped her up. We were both panting. A large athletic woman in some kind of uniform sprinted around a corner and pounced on us. "Got them," she said into a shoulder mic. "Now, girls, calm down. We're Protective Services. We're here to take you somewhere safe until you get a new home."

"Liver!" Tal shrieked. She kicked the woman in the shins and took off. I followed just far enough to hit a curb after Lady Godzilla snagged the back of my denim jacket. My cheek bruised, my palms scraped, I watched Tal be scooped up. Shouts and scuffling sounds from the ER lot indicated that Mr. Sam was putting up the best fight an ancient old man armed with hallucinations and deep love for our family could manage. Tears slid down my face when I heard him make a pained noise. And then, silence.

Lady Godzilla held me by the collar as we walked over. My heart fell at the sight of Mr. Sam sprawled limply on the pavement. A gurney was already being rushed out to him. And over to one side of the lot, two beefy men led Gus out of the hedges with a tight grip on his arms. His face was scratched, and he was struggling.

If this is how kids are protected, they should just set us loose in the woods, instead.

"Where are we going?" I demanded. They led us to the same car, thank goodness.

"A foster care home. You'll be fine."

"Our mother has a cousin up in the Crossroads Cove," Gus shouted. "She's famous. Delta Whittlespoon. Her husband's the deputy sheriff of Jefferson County. Call her. She'll take us."

"That has to be sorted out by a judge at a hearing."

I wrenched around as they opened car doors. "What about Mr. Sam? He's hurt."

"He'll get help. He needs to be evaluated. He's a danger to himself."

"Ralph!" Tal cried. "Our dog!"

"I'm sure you have neighbors who —"

"Then call them," Gus shot back. "Goddammit. Call Charlie Bowen, Sergeant Charlie Bowen, Asheville P.D."

"Shut your mouth, you little heathen." Gus got pushed into the back seat. Tal was handed in next. As I was being steered that way, a long, low dark car, like the kind you see in mobster movies, pulled in. A sensation jolted me. Chocolate with Reese's cups. Biscuits. And smoked pickles. "Jay!" I screamed.

I launched myself in that direction. Lady Godzilla grabbed me. I kept yelling his name as she wrestled me into the car. At any second, he'd hop out and race over to help. Why else would he have come? Who was he with? He must be here to help.

"Liver, liver, liver," Tal chanted, crying. As I crashed into the back seat next to her and

Gus, I met my brother's angry eyes.

"It's Jay out there," I moaned.

Gus nodded. "And he's with his uncle."

Jay

I saw Gabs, I heard her calling me. I pounded the tinted windows, wrestled the locked door, yelled. Sitting beside me, E.W. said in a calm tone, "I hate to say this, but you did this to her. And to her brother and sister. And to their mother. The damage can't be undone, not now."

I flung myself at him, fists swinging. But he was a large, powerfully-built man, who ran and lifted weights and sparred with a boxing trainer every morning. He cuffed me along the jaw and pinned me against the deep leather seat, pressing a forearm across my throat. "Here's what happens next," he said. "They're going far away from here. It's time you put their influence aside. If you cooperate, I'll make sure they end up in good homes. If not . . ." He let the implication dangle. Then he added, "The mining rights. I want your word."

I was dying inside. Revenge took the place of every other thought. *I can't trust him. I can't.* I'd find some way to take care of Gabs, Gus and Tal. I swore I would. We were in this nightmare together. I hoped they'd understand. I hoped Gabs would forgive me.

"The mining rights," E.W. repeated.

"No," I said.

Gabby

Relax, Gabby. I like little fat girls. You don't want to wake up your sister, do you?

His name doesn't matter. He was fourteen, one of our foster "brothers" among ten luckless boys and girls from six to sixteen; the bunk beds in the girls' rooms sagged in the middle and smelled funny, the food was processed junk, heavy on starches and cheap cuts of meat. The house was old and drafty, set somewhere on the rolling land east of the mountains. E.W. had made sure we were hidden from Delta, Sergeant Charlie, and anyone else who was demanding to know where Jane and Stewart Mac-Bride's kids had been sent and why an "undisclosed location" was needed to keep us safe from Mr. Sam, who was locked up in the dementia ward of an Asheville nursing home.

After a month of being cornered and groped during Tal's afternoon nap times — I wasn't about to leave her sleeping alone in the girls' rooms, because when she cried they locked her in a closet — I felt as if I'd never be clean again. Inside or out. I developed a habit of vomiting in the bathroom after meals. It made me feel in control of my body. That's all I cared about. To feel something resembling control. And to not think about Mama, Daddy, or Jay.

Gus looked like hell, too. I knew he was getting pushed around and punched by the older guys, including the same one who was grabbing me. My worst fear was that my attacker would taunt Gus with it.

There were some givens about Daddy's children in general and his son in particular.

We would kill people who did what that guy did to me.

Jay

Every day I asked, "Will you tell Delta where the MacBrides are?" Delta had practically stormed the house. There had been lawyers, confrontations. Sergeant Charlie and a lot of officers were mad as hell. People were talking, and pressure was building on DFACs to explain my uncle's influence.

But every day, so far, when I asked with brittle formality about Gabs's fate, Uncle E.W. had said, "I would like to see a two-thousand word essay on the Five Sisters Mine. Tell me about feldspar." Or, "Write me an article about the use of mica in electrical generators." Some days it was, "How many push-ups did you do with the trainer?" And others it was, "Tell Arlton (his assistant) I want your hair cut shorter than that, next time."

A little stab under the fingernails, every day. And my response was to say, "Yes, sir." And let it go at that. On top of E.W.'s little tortures, I dealt with my cousin Denoto, thirteen years old, E.W.'s oldest daughter. Her mother was long gone. Dark-haired, mean, sadistic, psycho, desperate to please E.W. and happy to share the misery of living under E.W.'s high-pressure thumb, she threw my books in the koi pond, called me names, and did everything short of poison me.

On the other hand, her half-sister, Quincy, whose mother was also a no-show, was a frail blond fairy, about fifteen but looking younger, whose pathological shyness included obsessive compulsive disorder, panic attacks, and regular trips to therapists and psychiatrists. Once she realized I was not going to make fun of her she darted around the shadows of the big Tudor house with stereo headphones over her ears and the disconnected wires dangling around her. She went from one tape player to another in the rooms, floating and touching her talisman spots repeatedly.

Uncle E.W. ignored her, the way you ignore a butterfly until it gets in your way.

I guess that's how she overheard so much. One day she flittered into the library where I was staring at a book on minerals and only thinking about Gabs, Gus, and Tal. Tap tap tap on the desk, tap tap tap on my arm, and then she slid a little piece of notepaper in front of me.

Tap tap tap on my shoulder, and she fluttered back out.

I stared at the address on it.

I couldn't use a phone; the housekeeping staff monitored everything I did. But I took a walk in the back garden, where a walled courtyard let in light through the slats of a granite frieze. I laid the slip of paper there with some sunflower seeds on top. My place for feeding the squirrels.

And leaving notes for Lawyer George.

Gabby

It wasn't our food magic that outted my secret to Gus, it was the plain old smell of vomit, two nights in a row, after dinner. He halted in the dingy hallway as I passed him, his shoulders rigid, his face going tight. A swollen spot bulged above his left eyebrow, and he had a tough edge in his eyes like he'd grown two years for every week we'd been there. I stopped too. It was a no-shit moment. We shared an ability that conveyed intuitions that went far beyond scent-auras, favorite foods and sweet-sour personality tests.

He searched my face, sniffing the awful odor. The instant an image — and scent — filled my mind, I saw it filling his, too. *Bruised peaches.* He growled like a dog in pain and slammed his hands into the wall on either side of me. I slapped him. "We're in the middle of nowhere. We can't call for help! Where would we go? And what if they catch us and divide us up? We can't risk doing that to Tal!"

"We don't live like this! We don't put up with this! We're MacBrides! We fight back! What if he grabs Tal next?"

I sucked in a breath. *"I'll kill him."*

"We kill him together. Tonight. Or we leave. Tonight."

Gabby

Around midnight, with a bag of stolen groceries hanging around Gus's neck and a second one around mine, we held Tal's hands and slipped outside. It was a half-mile to a paved road through treeless pastures where beef cattle grazed, then twenty miles in either direction to a convenience store where we could call Sergeant Charlie or Delta.

We started walking. There was a new moon. April was about to pass into May. Insects sang. The two-lane was empty until around dawn, when trucks and cars started to come along. We had a clear view ahead and behind, so we lay down in the roadside ditches each time. There was no other cover.

The plan worked fine until right around daylight. We spotted a big RV coming towards us. "Incoming," Gus said. We climbed down into a ditch. This one was soggy and littered with beer cans. Tal whimpered as we sank down in the chilly water. We were now cold, wet, filthy, and still at least two miles from a phone.

After the RV was well past, Gus craned his head to check the distance between us and it. When I heard the breath gush out of him I jerked upright. "Backing up," he said.

Three kids in the middle of isolated farm country at dawn. Just walking home from a spend-the-night-party? Gus and I traded a despairing look. Tal rested her forehead against my arm. "Maybe they'll be nice people," she said. "We can tell them we want to go live with Delta."

"No matter what happens from here on

out," I said to her and Gus, "we'll take care of each other, and if we ever get away from here, we're never coming back. North Carolina isn't home anymore."

He tilted his head. *Agreed.*

The RV, puffing diesel fumes, backed up to us and creaked to a halt. The door popped open.

Sergeant Charlie jumped out. Followed by Delta and Pike.

"Ralph, Ralph Ralph," Ralph said, leaping higher than any heart but ours.

Jay

FOUND THEM.
WE SENT THEM OUT OF STATE.
HIDDEN FROM E.W.
SAFE. DELTA KNOWS WHERE.

I tore Lawyer George's note into tiny pieces and scattered it under the roses. It would be a long time before I could find out more details about the where, the how of that rescue. If E.W. could find them, he'd have used them as pawns, hurt them again. I had to stay away, let Gabs go, for now. I doubt E.W. ever intended to send Gabs, Gus and Tal to Delta. He would have let them fade into the foster care system, be separated, be destroyed completely. Mr. Sam was locked up, but E.W. couldn't care less about his fate, so he let Delta take him to the Cove. He died there, a year later, wandering around Free Wheeler.

At least Gabs and the others were okay. I didn't know how much damage had been done to them already.

And how much damage had been done to me.

"Straithern School," E.W. said, tossing a severely crimped binder on his desk. Every crisp movement and acidic tinge to his voice said he knew I'd found a way to help the MacBrides. "Several of our stellar Wakefield men have attended," he said. "Those who need structure, discipline. It's a military-style program. Extremely high academic standards, but also demanding personal protocols and, well, it will make a man out of you. It certainly took the rebellion out of me, when I was your age. I was hoping to avoid passing the lesson along. Enjoy."

That fall I looked out the barracks window at a drill field outside Raleigh in the heart of the Carolina flatlands. My head was shaved, I'd already been beaten up three times by older classmen, and I'd seen my weaker peers reduced to pissing themselves in hazing rituals that weren't meant to make men out of boys, just sadistic lords of industry out of the survivors. A Wakefield had founded the school in 1892. Four generations had attended, including E.W.

At least I could get mail from Lawyer George, now. He'd been disbarred, but was setting up an office. Part of Dad's fall-back plan had been a fund to pay his salary in case he got sacked. So George was organizing the bones of the company I would run, one day. *Be strong, Jay. Vickie and I love you. You'll see Gabs again one day.*

I WROTE BACK: *I'll find her, and I'll destroy E.W.*

I didn't want to be loved. I wanted to be feared.

Part Two

2012
Gabby in Los Angeles

On the eve of Christmas Eve, I'd learn whether enough evidence existed to frame me for embezzlement.

"The operative word in John Michael Michael's charges against you is 'bossy'," my attorney said. "So when you face the judge, try to act . . ." Her voice trailed off as she looked up at me. "I'll visit you in prison," she finished.

"I was his chef. His managing partner. The boss. I was supposed to be bossy. How could I be anything but bossy when my movie-star investor was doing his best to steal all the profits?"

"Let me do the talking, please? We can't dispute the assault charge. You stabbed him in the ass with a pickle fork. That's a given. So now let's concentrate on the embezzlement charge."

"I. Did. Not. Steal. One. Penny."

I'm a MacBride.

"I know that, Gabby. And we're going to keep digging until we prove he skimmed the money. In the meantime . . ."

Her voice faded in my ears. *My reputation will be ruined. I'll never get another investor. Never get hired as a chef again. I'll have to tell Tal and Gus that this mess is far worse than the pickle-fork incident. It's going to hit the tabloids. Their sister, the thief.*

"Excuse me," a lawyerly voice called. We turned to watch a crisp platoon of dark-suited lawyers wearing shiny pastel ties — the women, too — heading toward us.

John Michael Michael's hit squad. My attorney whispered, "Look at those poker faces. Something's up. They're not happy. It's good for us."

Lead Attorney stopped inches from her, while the others circled the wagons, watching for roving spies from the *National Enquirer.* "You're tougher than you look," he said to her. "Vicious. Come and see me about a position."

"Thanks, but I never sign job contracts in blood."

My mind filled with the scent of avocado and lemon. Her safe place, as usual. But . . . wait a minute. Something was new. A dash

100

of *pico de huh*? She didn't know what the hell he was getting at, and neither did I, but we'd play along.

"Would you really go public with that dirt?" he asked. He glanced at me. "You're a ball-breaker, I've heard that much. But you'd ruin him over this? Hurt his family?"

My mind whirled. John Michael Michael didn't have a lot of secrets. Drug use, girlfriends, boyfriends, wild parties, a fetish for pickles. How much worse could it get? Except for the pickle fetish. Nothing wrong with that.

"Don't answer that," my attorney said. To Lead Lawyer she said, "You're offering us something?"

"We'll drop everything. The assault charge, the embezzlement accusations. Just walk away."

After a stunned moment in which she and I traded poker-faced "Hmmm's," while inside I squealed and thanked my angels and cried, she turned to him and said, "We want a public statement saying it was a misunderstanding and he has nothing but respect and affection for Gabby, and that as soon as she opens a new restaurant he'll be one of her first customers."

"After what you threatened to tell the world about his elderly mother and the monkey?" He looked from her to me. "Congratulations, ladies. You make me feel dirty. I'd forgotten what the sensation is like."

My god. Even *my* attorney looked at me with a queasy question in her eyes. I waved a hand. "Just say we had a misunderstanding."

"It's a deal."

I was being freed not by truth, justice and the American way, but by a brutal tactic cooked up by a mysterious someone who didn't care who got hurt on my behalf.

Once we were alone in a corner my attorney said, "Do you have a friend in the Mafia? The CIA? The NSA? The Taliban?"

My chest turned into a battleground between two hearts, one squeezing down into a hard knot of resistance and anger, one swelling up with pleasure.

Jay.

This favor was going to cost me. Wakefields never did anything for free. Five minutes later, my phone began vibrating. The text message had an eight-two-eight area code. Asheville, North Carolina.

Payback time.

Jay

The Bright Crimson Stain of Regret

Christmas Card from Delta to Jay

Listen to me this time, Jay, or lose Gabby —
and your soul — once and for all, the Christmas card began. *CHANGE THE WORLD*
FOR THE BETTER — NOT JUST IN LITTLE
WAYS BUT IN BIG ONES!!! The Dalai Lama
said that. Or maybe it was Dolly Parton. Either
way, I agree.

I liked how Delta used wit and subtlety to
make a point. Not.

In the light of a single bleak work lamp
hung up by the construction crew, my red
fingerprints looked like smeared roses on
the card's pale innards. I stood in the
haunted confines of the P, B and S Building. When E.W. controlled it, he let it go to
hell, just to taunt me. When I turned twenty-
one, that changed. I tracked Gabby to
California. It didn't go so well. Actually,
parts of it were the best three days of my
life. The rest were the worst three days of
my life. She never wanted to see me again.
Gus had joined the army. Tal was in college.

None of them wanted to come back to
North Carolina, ever. Certainly not for me.
Not for the man I'd become. Never mind
that survival had required it. I'd been left

behind to fend for myself, while they had each other and Delta. Maybe they romanticized what life with money was like.

Maybe I'd just romanticized my time at the P, B, and S Diner.

In the years since then, I'd let local nonprofit groups use the space for free. Lest anyone think I'd gone soft, I got a nice tax write-off out of it — and a hard-nosed reputation for rounding up street kids who camped out in the cellar. My trap-and-release program steered them to some of the same groups who used the upstairs for fundraising.

Some of them weren't grateful. Like tonight. My blood, from the unfortunate scuffle with a certain headstrong mime, slid down the glittering edge of Delta's oversized holiday card. Never try to help a mime. Especially not a street performer in Asheville.

Not even when he was my own cousin. Quincy's son.

I ignored the sting and looked at Delta's words. She didn't just write to me, she sent homey lectures, set down on paper in her impossibly gravy-flavored scrawl; she grabbed me by my shirtfront and shook me. She'd appreciate my bleeding on her Santa Claus on this night, one eve before Christmas Eve, while waiting for Gabs to arrive in the mist of a cold Appalachian December.

I still despised Uncle E.W., but I'd learned a lot from the years under his thumb. Wakefields provide the counterpoint to the gauzy, fragile world of wishful thinking. We build infrastructure. We create jobs. We put money into everyone's banks. We're the grown-ups in the playground.

You can't take care of the helpless if you're helpless, too.

You can make things right, Jay. You've got to tell Gabby the truth about Free Wheeler. That it should belong to her and her brother and sister. Why you won't let go of it.

"I only know parts of the truth," I said aloud. "And the truth is overrated as a solution to big problems." Ten years earlier, I'd shared a chunk of my truth with Gabs. Told her I'd had no choice but to fight E.W. Trusting him to keep his word wasn't an option. But what she heard was this: I'd chosen to protect Free Wheeler instead of her.

I walked out into the chilly North Carolina night and turned to padlock the building's weathered door. Decorative street lamps, bow-tied with greenery and red bows, marched up the hill past small ornamental shade trees that had rooted between the old pavers, their bare branches frail in the misty light. A young musician, armed with a guitar, a china-eyed dog on a braided-hemp leash, and a hummock of waxy blond dreads, spit on the aged diamond sidewalk pavers as I walked past. He didn't miss a beat, strumming *O Holy Night,* on his six-string.

I dropped several twenties in the frayed guitar case by his feet. His dog wagged. Dogs trust me. I must not smell dastardly. Got them fooled, always have. Ever since Ralph.

"Blood money, Capitalist Tyrant," the dog's human said in a voice dripping with sarcasm.

Probably an art major with a minor in Getting Stoned. We had a lot of UNCA students working the city as bartenders, wait staff, sales clerks and street performers, along with runaways and hardened street people from all over the county. They shared two things in common: they loved this mecca of tolerant oddity, and they hated Wakefields.

"Nice dog," I said. "Looks tasty."

The guitarist's dreadlocks stood on end. "Meat eater!" he yelled.

True. My vegetarian days were long gone. I headed up the sidewalk. He didn't kick my cash down the nearest sewer grate. They never did. No one looked past the suit and my name. That was fine by me. At least for a little while longer. Long enough to hang E.W. the same way he'd ousted George. I knew more about E.W. than E.W. knew these days. And he knew a helluva lot less about me than he had any idea. A few more mistakes in judgment by E.W. would be enough leverage. It had to be enough.

My gaze rose to the gray-cold night sky, searching for pinpoints of light, comfort. I wasn't looking for meaning, a sense that a bigger power in the world existed to offer redemption. No. Only looking for Gabby. Greta Garbo MacBride. Forgiveness only mattered if it came from her.

Gabs's plane is landing now.

History was closing in. The past was here. The MacBrides were coming home. First Tal, and now Gabby. She'd finally agreed to see me in person again. She and Tal thought I wanted to gut Free Wheeler of everything except its historical facades, turn the buildings into boutiques and restaurants, build a hotel and golf course, and put up gates everywhere. Plus hire them as chefs. My employees. Wakefield underlings. Under my control. Just like their parents had been. I'd partner with investors, tie up multiple interests in long-term property leases on the buildings and the business management contracts.

That's what I wanted them to think. What I wanted everyone in western North Carolina to believe. What E.W. and everyone in his inner circle definitely believed by now. E.W. was convinced I wasn't bluffing. He saw his chances of carving up that piece of mountain land dwindling in the face of a massive development being perched atop his prized quartz.

So he was getting more careless. Taking more risks.

Or, as Delta put it after she went to him with proof that Arlo Claptraddle and Sam Osserman were the same person, and Sam was, indeed, Gabs, Tal and Gus's grandfather, making them the heir to Free Wheeler — and just how much was E.W. willing to pay her to keep that a secret, because maybe she'd have a change of heart about that mining access one day and not want to share it with a pack of Nettie descendants — "You'd think he'd have heard my bra picking up radio stations with all the FBI wires I was wearing."

I was catching him in one fraud at a time, a lie here, a law broken there.

Like grains of quartz sand, eventually they

would form a mountain.

My hand throbbed, just like the rest of me, my mind blood-red, my body stained with the tactics I'd learned, the things I was willing to do. I was bleeding for Gabby, and she was worth it.

Gabby
Look Homeward, Greta Garbo MacBride

I drove a rented sedan from the Asheville airport in heavy shopping traffic, pushing the accelerator too hard in the gloom of early pre-Christmas Eve, thinking about Tal's acceptance of our childhood home with its sad memories and her happy new life in this part of the mountains people called the Land of the Sky. Tal had come back here and was instantly seduced. Not me. Not Gus. Wouldn't happen.

You can never go home again.

I pulled into the parking lot of a tall hotel within easy walking distance of downtown. My finger hovered over my phone, listening to the Thomas Wolfe audiobook for a few more seconds.

The mountains were his masters. They rimmed in life. They were the cup of reality, beyond growth, beyond struggle and death. They were his absolute unity in the midst of eternal change.

It hit me: *I'm going to stand face-to-face with eternal change. Hear Jay's voice, look up into his eyes, and want to touch him.* After our adult reunion in California, I swore this moment would never happen. But every day since then I'd thought about him, and every night.

I looked over the tops of the bare trees around the lot's perimeter. A gray night. The mountains were hidden in mists. When I opened the car door, the wind smelled like home, like Mama and Daddy and pickles. Like the hard, cold facts.

Jay had been broken in the soft places. So had I. I'd hardened into a proud MacBride — no retreat, no surrender.

He'd turned into a Wakefield. Someone who'd win at all costs. That painful truth sank in thirteen years ago, after our weekend together. Me, eighteen. Him, twenty-one. He'd confessed that he'd let me, Tal and Gus be thrown into that foster care home rather than give up a meaningless piece of land to his uncle. He was just a kid when it happened, sure, under pressure and without many choices. But at least *he'd* had a choice.

I told him about *mine.*

Relax, Gabby. I like little fat girls.

Jay
The Piano Loft Is Still a Lonely Home

I paced in front of a twenty-foot high wall of shelves filled with Dad's books. Rows of paperbacks, each filled with dog-eared novels I'd preserved inside clear, archival-quality binders that let the wild glory of their covers show through. Space monsters and Tarzan, gunslingers and hard-boiled detectives. Bodacious babes, too, of course. In spaceships, or being clutched by swamp monsters, or screaming in the arms of gangsters, but almost always arching their backs as they ran, in slitted skirts and high heels, from the win-the-damsel-in-distress fantasies of boy-men everywhere.

"She took an earlier connection out of Atlanta, sir. I'm sorry. She escaped me. She's been at the hotel for an hour already. I found this at the airport. They paged me, and I went to Security. It was . . . embarrassing."

George held out a gift box containing a fat glass jar full of Gabs's homemade pickles. "The note says, 'Dear George, You still like garlic okra.' It's uncanny, sir."

The "sir" habit had slipped into place in my early twenties. I didn't ask Lawyer George to call me that. But I didn't tell him to stop, either. I kept a distance between myself and even those closest to me. Which was why Gabs wouldn't come home with me ten years ago. She said home wasn't home. She said I wasn't there anymore.

"Nothing for me?"

"This, sir." He pulled another box from his man-purse. Vickie and one of their grandkids had bought it for him on his sixtieth birthday. I kept threatening to buy him matching pumps.

I pulled a silver ribbon off the box and opened it. Inside a crushed barricade of gold tissue, my jar of pickles shimmered like toxic waste. Red, spikey and angry looking.

They needed ointment.

Gabby's note said, *I'll meet you at Foxgloves Pub, seven* P.M.

I resisted an urge to stroke her handwriting.

She really is here. In Asheville. Within reach.

"Sir?" George touched a thick finger to his ear bud. He looked like an oversized dwarf from *The Hobbit,* listening. Then, "She's left the hotel. In tonight's traffic, it could take her fifteen minutes to drive to the pub. Would you like me to call a car for you?"

So much for my invitation to meet me at my private enclave — *Wakefield's,* the restaurant I owned, downstairs.

All right, dammit. On to the alternate plan. The pub was only two blocks from here. Maybe I could relax her with good beer from Asheville's many breweries, drop a trail of dill chips, and lure her this way.

"I'll walk."

"Is that wise? Quincy's son is not carrying a pretend knife. You need stitches. If Donny attacks you again, you may need more."

"I'll take my chances. If he attacks, I'll at least know where he is."

George nodded at the thick band of tape and gauze around the palm of my left hand. "Are you sure I shouldn't call the doctor? Or send a bodyguard with you?"

"I'm going by instinct. Let's not give E.W. any excuse to pay attention to me. Just keep looking for them."

Donny — short for Elladon, yes, the elf from Lord of the Rings — was the brother of Arwen, yes, the elf princess, et cetera. Quincy's fragile mental state had carried her away on a cloud, and E.W. put her in a nice facility near her favorite place, Disney World, in Orlando. The father of her twins was unknown. Arwen and Donny were supposed to be in a boarding school here in Asheville, but they'd escaped recently, as if sensing that their grandfather was only waiting for an excuse to send them far, far away,

113

just as he tried to send Gabs, Gus and Tal.

It was my mission to catch them before he did.

I ditched my pinstriped suit for outdoor gear and wound one of Lucy Parmenter's beautiful wool scarves around my neck. *The scarf fairy,* they called her up in the Cove. Fragile, unable to fight back effectively. Her vulnerable sweetness made me think of my father. Not all the Wakefield men were sons of bitches. "Where's Dustin?"

"On the prowl. He's looking for them, too."

"Find him."

"I know. All hands on deck. We will."

Dustin was Cousin Denoto's boy. She'd battled E.W. in an epic daughter-father war since those teen years when she used me as her surrogate punching bag. In some twisted way she adored him but couldn't earn his respect, because daughters didn't belong in the mining business, at least in his view of tradition. Her job was to produce grandsons he could groom as heirs, in case I never suc-cumbed to his brainwashing.

So Denoto married E.W.'s hand-picked husband, and fell in love with him, unfortu-nately. He cheated on her constantly and left the day Dustin was born. The battle over Dustin's future began immediately, with

Denoto recognizing that she finally had bartering power with her father, and a way to capture both his attention and his respect, as the perfect mother to his backup heir.

Then I hit my stride, and George and I unveiled the *coup de Wakefield* we'd plotted for years: TWSon (Tom Wakefield Son) outbid E.W. on four mines he'd thought were his for the asking price. We also delivered inside information on Wakefield Mining to every regulatory agency, union and watchdog group. E.W. spent the next five years paying hefty fines and settling lawsuits. Dustin became the sole focus of his heirdom, and he shoved Denoto aside. Not just shoved, but destroyed her.

Suddenly a team of doctors were questioning her mental stability. Everyone knew she was bi-polar, but it was controlled by medication. The more they probed, insinuated, and smeared her, the more she unraveled. E.W.'s tactics broke her. One court order later, and Dustin was under E.W.'s control.

That's when Denoto joined the rebel forces up in the Little Finn, where my cousin Will Bonavendier had established a crazy colony of Wakefield-hating doomsday preppers. The fact that they wanted to eliminate mining, fracking, the gas industry, the coal industry, capitalism, industrialism, and about a hundred other "isms" could be summed up in their goal to ruin E.W. Wakefield. I appreciated all of that, except for the fact that some of them included me on the enemies list.

In the battle between the mining conglomerate and the ragtag rebels with a cause, Dustin wasn't sure which side to choose. E.W. had played nice with him, in counterpoint to his mother trying to control him in her own way. He didn't know his grandfather well enough to run like hell, yet. But there was an allure to the off-the-grid world of the Little Finn lifestyle. A young man with rebellion in his DNA could find much to admire in Bonavendier's agenda.

E.W., naturally, had a problem with his grandson being courted by Jedi tree huggers, and E.W. was now preparing to ship him off to Straithern for hardcore manly indoctrination.

Dustin was clueless. Fortunately, I was not going to let that happen. I could feel my teeth grinding as I made for the door.

George sighed. "Good luck, sir. With the kids. And with Gabby." He cradled his jar of Gabs's pickles. "She's got a knack with sugar and vinegar."

I set my pickled peppers on the finely-grained wood of my very large desk. The jar squatted there morosely, its red cayenne innards looking like shriveled hearts.

Gabby

Asheville was packed with Christmas spirit, which, to me, was the scent of cinnamon. The whole downtown looked like a shaken Christmas globe of decorated historic-registry buildings and modern gentry under mountain skies. Gothic with a side dish of Bohemian.

My face prickled with dew. On a six-foot, size-eighteen woman whose inner thighs rub together, personal moisture is not delicate and dewy. My makeup, hair, all the fine-tuned "look" I'd put in place for meeting Jay, all of it was heading south like thin caramel on a hot fudge sundae.

I let the rented sedan meander toward the wide elegance of Biltmore Avenue — procrastinating, dodging the shoppers in holiday outfits, the happy, happy couples and perfect families coming out of the restaurants — trying to replace the mental slide-show of my 1990-ish memories on its comfortably shabby, historic, bohemian streets with the gentrified Asheville of twenty-two years later.

I avoided Lexington's siren call toward

the old P, B and S Diner building. I tried not to think of West Asheville. Jay had bought Mama and Daddy's house, along with sections of the entire community. He'd preserved it. Offered the house to me during our weekend together, along with a deed for the P, B and S building. All I had to do was come home. His love was a trade. Everything was a contract. Strings attached. He couldn't understand why I didn't accept.

Bright lights. No empty storefronts. Pack Square had sprouted a huge abstract fountain, like a giant flat bowl. At the base of the Vance monument were life-sized bronze sculptures of pigs and turkeys, perpetually reminding people that an intersection of drovers' trails put Asheville on the map in the late 1700s. Someone had tied red bows on the turkeys' necks.

I saw fewer tattoo parlors and black-windowed alt-music clubs. I saw lots more luxury cars, lots more luxury people. Correction: lots more people but still plenty of tats, dreads, piercings, with Goths, Emos, Wiccans and Other Alternative Lifestyles among the suburban types. The crowds streamed in happy unison, going with the holiday flow. They took the off ramps into sushi bars, organic coffee shops, boutiques and art galleries. A line had formed outside the tiny Fine Arts Theater, waiting to buy tickets for the latest foreign or indie film.

The street performers grabbed me by the heart. The kids working tonight weren't students gathering anecdotes for an essay in class. They needed money. Badly.

The Rodriquez family, anchored by an L.A. police officer who was a friend of a friend in the network of law officers Sergeant Charlie trusted, had adopted me, Tal and Gus once we fled foster care and went to California. The Rodriquezes ran a chain of Tex-Mex restaurants. Family business. They worked sixteen-hour days, their children worked, their aunts, uncles and cousins worked. Me, Tal and Gus, the only pale-faced redheads in the Rodriquez clan, bussed tables, washed dishes, prepped food, swept floors . . . and I, being tall, chunky and burrito-shaped, donned the costume the L.A. Times food columnist called, "the kitschy mascot of one of the best indie chains in the city."

I spent several of my most formative late-teenage years inside that synthetic burrito suit. I appeared at store openings, *Cinco de Mayo* celebrations, fundraisers for charities, and promotional events of all kinds. I waved my lettuce-leaf hands at passing traffic, tap-danced in my squishy tomato-wedge shoes, and peered out at the world, sweating and itchy, through a thin gauze of fabric hidden among foam-stuffed black olives and bouncing foam tufts of shredded cheese.

So I knew how hard it was to work the street. To get strangers to pay attention. How it feels being punched in the knees by children while their parents snap photos, being laughed at by teenagers, spit on by drunks, stared at, insulted, asked for blow jobs, pitied, pushed and, maybe worst of all, ignored.

I whipped the car into the only empty parking space in front of the old piano factory, now covered in a new granite façade with an elegantly-lit sign above the restaurant that filled the bottom floor. Wakefield's. A uniformed doorman kept the riffraff away. I looked up at the dark, tall windows of the loft above.

The Foxgloves Pub was still two blocks away, but I'd never find another open spot. *It's fate. Cruel fate.*

My phone beeped. An email from Tal.

Where r u? I keep getting your vinegar aroma, worse than before. TROUBLE. Please call or text. Keep saying to yourself, CATCH WAKEFIELDS WITH

HONEY, NOT VINEGAR.
    Please?

                          Love you,
                          Tal

I rolled down my window and sucked cold air into my lungs. The sidewalks were crowded. Chatter and Christmas carols filled my ears.

A sound like a strangled goose made me jump. A few paces up the sidewalk, a silver elf blew hard into a badly tuned clarinet. As I got out of the car, another ear-shivering squawk filled the air, driving a wedge in the pedestrians.

'Hurrah hurrah, huzzah hooray!" he shouted. "Welcome to a performance by Lady Overjoy and Donny Malaprop!"

Tips Kindly Appreciated was posted on a plastic bucket spray-painted with glitter. Donny began playing *Jingle Bells* on the clarinet. Horribly. The Wakefield doorman spotted them and instantly reached for a phone.

Lady Overjoy, a silver fairy with lovely wire wings and a silver gown, perched delicately on a wooden pallet draped in matching gauze. She posed without blinking, without flinching in the clammy cold. I watched as a woman dropped a dollar in

121

the bucket. Lady Overjoy pivoted gracefully toward the giver and curtsied. But other people streamed past her and the elf without a glance. Who had time to toss a dollar at a bad clarinetist and a thin silver fairy looking cold?

I pulled a twenty out of my purse, slapped invisible wrinkles out of my black pants and long gray coat, locked the car, then kicked a fake-croc pump against the steel post of a parking meter. In the old days a good kick might jar a nickel loose or bounce the needle up an hour. But now a high-tech robo-meter just stared back at me, waiting. I slashed a credit card through its evil slit, set the time for two hours, then kicked the post again.

Lady Overjoy screamed.

The Wakefield doorman had pounced, but he wasn't alone. A security guard pinned the elf against the Wakefield building's sleek black granite. Lady Overjoy ripped off her wire wings and began flogging the guard and the doorman, who tried to wave her off while dodging a serious whisking. "Got you, Donny," he said loudly.

"Please let him go," she begged, hugging her ruined wings to her gown. "We don't want to go back to boarding school. We hate it."

"Then why did you pick Mr. Wakefield's building? You're just asking to get caught."

"I want to see Jay. We're just waiting for Jay."

"Well, McStabby the Mime has already seen him."

"What? When?"

"Halp. Hep. Heh," the clarinet elf squeaked.

"You're hurting him. He can't breathe!"

"Tell him to calm down. Mr. Wakefield gave orders to get him and you off the streets. Period."

Was this what Jay had sunk to? Throwing teenage street performers off the sidewalks in front of his building?

I pushed my way through the gawkers. "Let the elf go."

"Ma'am, mind your own business."

The clarinet elf was turning purple.

"You're strangling him."

"Please," Lady Overjoy begged the men. "I told him not to go see Jay alone. I begged Donny. We won't come back. I swear."

"He assaulted Mr. Wakefield."

I snorted. "With a clarinet?"

"Lady, this is family business. Please!"

The elf's eyes rolled to the whites. He kicked weakly, his cheap, silver-hued jogging shoes drumming the security guard's tailored legs.

Lady Overjoy lunged at the security guard. "You're killing him!"

He shoved her. She fell back, sprawling on the cold pavement, her cheap, gauzy gown flying up to reveal gray leggings and soggy slippers with torn toes.

I reached into my purse. *Are you crazy? Don't get involved, you've just been cleared of assault with a deadly fork in California. Jay's lawyers got you off. You owe him.*

I pulled out a slick little device I'd bought back when I was catering So Cal parties where the patrons thought helping themselves to "the help" was a perk of the event.

Putting my thumb on the button, I pointed it at the security guard, while the sidewalk crowd shrieked and ran. "Let the elf go."

When he ignored me, I Tasered him.

Heading for the Yellow Lights

Donny and Lady Overjoy huddled in the back seat, texting on their phones and talking in coded nerd language. I couldn't decipher it. However, the Lady's tragic sighs and Donny's outraged grunts couldn't hide their emotional hunger from me.

She's the dependable brine. He is the over-saturated spices. Plain tomato relish versus jalapeño chow chow.

"What did you do to Jay Wakefield?" I asked, steering the rental car up an off-ramp they pointed out.

"Nothing much. He'll live," Donny said. "Too bad."

I jerked the car to a halt on an emergency lane then twisted to face them. Lady Overjoy looked exhausted and worried. Donny looked like a cornered miniature rooster. A silver one with a striped elf shirt. "Don't make me come back there," I said. "Talk."

"I accidentally nicked him on the hand."

"Define 'nicked.' "

"With my knife." He pulled out a pocket combo so old that the Swiss Army emblem had faded to a swish. "He's okay."

My chest expanded in relief. Jay wasn't badly hurt.

"Donny didn't mean to hurt him," the Lady said wistfully.

He snorted. "Yes, I did."

She winced. "Please, just drop us off in front of the primitive yoga studio up there in that shopping center. The one with the yellow security lights. Someone's coming to meet us."

"Where will you go?"

She put a silver hand on the sleeve of my coat, begging. I saw myself at her age.

"Please don't ask questions. We take care of ourselves."

"I can help you. Trust me. I've been where you are."

"You're surrounded by spirits," Donny said suddenly. His silver brow wrinkling, he leaned forward, scanning me with an awed expression. "Old ones. From all around here. They're glad you're back. You're the second one they've been waiting for. But you're not the last."

A chill went up my spine.

"Please," Lady Overjoy whispered. "My . . . Donny . . . he thinks he knows things. He reads strange sites on the Internet. He has an imagination. I take care of him. I get him his . . . medications. I promise."

"I do know things." Donny said. "I know you won't hurt us; that's why we got into your car. I know you can feel what makes people hungry. But you're hungry, too." He paused. "Cousin Jay wants you to forgive him. But he has to die for you to do that."

"Cousin Jay?"

The blood drained out of my head. I made my lungs expand, willing my veins and arteries to put up road blocks. "Shusssh," the fairy hissed. "Ma'am, he's just kidding."

"No, I'm not." Donny sounded adamant.

"He has to die. It's his destiny. Because he loves you."

I turned back to the steering wheel and drove to the shopping center. The surroundings were stark, utilitarian, rimmed with treeless highway and exposed to the mountain-etched bowl of sky. Harsh yellow security lamps glared down. In front of the yoga studio in a strip of nondescript spaces set a muddy Land Rover. As soon as I pulled in beside it, the driver's door opened and a tall young man stepped out.

Lady and Donny bounded from my car and went to him.

I frowned, trying to analyze what was familiar about the stranger. His dark, nearly black hair was swept sideways in a jaunty flash; he was in his mid-teens, but with a presence of self that seemed older. Cased in a quilted high-tech work jacket, jeans and lace-up lumberjack boots, he circled a long arm around Lady's waist, and she looked up at him with appreciation. *He looks like Jay. Another cousin or, dear God, not a secret son?*

I got out. He tried to blind me with a smile, but it suddenly stalled. "You're her. The one Grandfather blames for messing with Jay's mind. Grandfather knows you're here."

"Whose side are you on?" the girl asked. "Our mother trusts Cousin Jay, but she's . . ."

"Like me," Donny said. "Not really living on this planet."

The tall one, the driver who resembled Jay, turned to them and said, "Let's go." To me he said, "Jay is glad you're here. Grandfather isn't. Which side are you on?"

A police siren cut through the lightly falling rain. Donny, Lady Overjoy, and their rescuer jumped in the SUV and left.

An Asheville PD cruiser blocked my Honda, followed by a second patrol car that zoomed up beside me, as if I might bolt for the steep slope at the edge of the parking lot, heading into the wilds of a drainage ditch.

The officers came toward me slowly, their hands on their holstered guns. "Hands up, and place them on top of your head," one ordered.

Was Jay having me arrested?

Welcome home.

Jay
Forces Are at Work

Why did Gabs have to stand me up in the back room of an Irish pub full of blinking Christmas lights and motion-sensitive Santa

Leprechauns that wiggled their asses and chirped, "Merry Christmas and Luck o' the Irish to ya!"

Every few minutes the customers up front at the bar came to the doorway to gaze longingly at the forbidden billiard tables. It didn't help that I looked like the kind of privileged man who takes toys away from the workers and gives them to his pets.

I lowered my phone long enough to say to George, "Buy everyone a round of drinks on my tab. And whatever they want to eat. Extra buffalo wings. Steaks. Lobster. Tater tots. And unplug the Santas. Or shoot them. Either option is fine by me." George nodded as he continued listening to his earpiece.

I walked to the back of the room, speaking in a low, calm voice into my cell. "Did she check out of her hotel?"

"No, sir." One of George's team was stationed at the Renaissance lobby.

"Stay there and keep watching."

I clicked to another call. "Did she return the rental?"

"No, sir."

"Ask your brother in airport security to get you inside the gate area for the next connecting flight to Los Angeles. Watch everyone who departs. If you're arrested as a terrorist threat, I'll pay for your defense."

"Yes, sir." He sighed, well-paid but un-happy.

I clicked to a third call, about to tell the leader of Team Sidewalk Search to sweep Lexington Avenue next. She might have headed for the P, B and S building. God, I hoped not. Revisiting her mother's eviction by Uncle E.W. wouldn't make a good start to the evening.

George tapped me on the shoulder. George isn't a tapper. I whirled around. He looked up at me grimly. "E.W. had her arrested."

Gabby
Gabby Cooks Up Trouble

"So if you mince the turkey meat, like this —" I diced the chilled breast meat with a police-approved plastic knife, while four of Daddy's other old cop buddies sat around a table in the police station's break room — "so that it's finely chopped enough to absorb the acidic flavor of the balsamic reduction, and then" — I mixed several handfuls of diced olives and celery into the meat, stirring with plastic spoons — "the oregano and the cumin will be pulled into the meat quicker, and the result will be the most flavorful turkey salad ever, not just spicy and well-seasoned, but with the edge that only a touch of culinary acid can give to food."

I set the large bowl among them, and they dug in with plastic sporks. One had loaned me a piece of his Tupperware from the potluck buffet set out along a wall under rows of mug shots.

I stood back, watching them "Uhmmm" and "Ah" with tears burning the backs of my eyes. I wiped my hands on paper towels. An over-sized Asheville P.D. t-shirt covered my gray pullover sweater and slacks. A gift from Daddy's pals, all of them burly and aging, gone gray and nearing retirement.

I saw Daddy as he would have become, in their ruddy faces, their weathered hands and spreading bellies. I had a deep affection for these men, who remembered young Stewart MacBride and his incredible wife, Jane, the best cook in Asheville.

A knock on the break room door made me flinch. Time to go back to my cell? I shivered. A childhood fear of windowless rooms made bile rise in my throat.

A grizzled sergeant poked his head inside.

"Sergeant Charlie!" I headed toward him with arms out, despite his scowl.

"Sssh, keep it down, sweetie pie." He gave me a quick bear hug while motioning for the others. In a low voice he said, "Got to move her out of here fast."

They leapt to their feet as if they were young men again. Charlie handed me my purse and coat, grabbed me by one elbow, and the other four formed a guard around me.

I gaped at them. "What the . . . where? Why?"

"Don't say nothing, just walk and look innocent," Charlie whispered.

They whisked me down several halls, then to an exit that led downstairs. Once we were clattering down the steps of a fire exit, Charlie told me, "You've got to trust Jay on this. Let him handle things. It's tricky with his cousin Will Bonavendier up in the Little Finn. If Will's hiding those kids . . ."

"Tricky?"

"Well, yeah. I'm not sure if Will and Jay are working together against E.W. or always about to kill each other. Just watch Jay's back."

"Jay wouldn't . . ." My stomach twisted. I couldn't be sure. Did I really know Jay?

We reached the bottom landing, and Charlie quickly unlocked a security door. I spun around, searching his face. "Would this Will Bonavendier really start a fight?"

"I don't know, hon, but if you still care

about Jay, just give him a chance to do whatever it is he's up to, all right?"

Charlie pivoted me toward the now-open door, which let in a blast of cold, damp, air. A starkly-lit world of parked police cars showed me nothing but a side street across from the historic brick edifice of Pack Tavern. Charlie pushed me gently out of the nest. "Maybe he's just trapped in the world he was born in, like the rest of us."

The door shut. The click of a high-tech bolt raised goose bumps on my arms.

I turned slowly toward the vaguely sinister side street with its shadowy corners and rows of patrol cars. Empty of human life. An engine came to life somewhere. Tires rolled on concrete, heading toward me. I backed up to the door, my mind racing. I needed a plan.

I just wanted to go back to the hotel, eat everything in sight, vomit, then head into the mountains above the city. I'd go to the Cove. Stay with Tal and her new love, Doug Firth. Hug my niece, Eve.

Helluva of way to surprise my baby sister and her future husband, but together we'd come up with some kind of plan. If Jay wanted to track me down, he'd have to send his mercenaries to the Cove to do it.

A hulking, camo-painted pickup truck

roared toward me. I was blinded by its headlights plus the search lights riding the roof like extra eyes on a large bug. Squinting, I noted a front winch, a thick roll bar over the cab, and enough mud on the sides to start a pottery.

The Armageddon Truck purred to a stop. Heavy diesel fumes oozed from the rumbling muffler. The window slid down with an electric whir.

Jay hung an elbow out, cased in a wolf-gray jacket with a Frankenstein line of crude stitches patching a tear in the padded forearm. I had warned myself in a thousand memories that he was a force of nature, six-foot-six-feet of extraordinary presence, and that the sexual energy that flowed between us would happen no matter what got in its way. But I was not prepared for this. I hurried down the steps, looking right and left, as if his entourage might leap from behind the foggy street lamps.

His darkly browed gaze, the silver stare of an unrepentant predator, scanned me as if I were bar-coded for inventory. A faded patch on the shoulder of his jacket said he'd climbed Mt. Everest. Probably to scope it out for a mining project.

There was no obvious emotion in his face, but a flash of urgency arced from him and hit me where I lived. Smoke curled from a fat cigar clenched in his teeth, drifting above the jacket's fleece collar. He blew it away with an air kiss that pursed his wide mouth; he even sniffed the air as if making sure the effect was headed in my direction. As a boy, he'd been aristocratic looking, but years of reckless adventure sports, combined with shoving his face into other people's business, had crumpled the bridge of his long nose and skewed the tip.

"What are you doing?" I asked. "What's your scheme, this time?"

The edge of his breath touched my face.

Jay reached for the cigar with long, blunt fingers that had thrown touchdowns for Duke yet could slip inside my body as gently as feathers stroking air. My eyes went to the wide strip of gauze and tape around his hand. On his palm, a pink stain seeped through.

He airlifted the stogie just long enough to say, "If you want to help save my cousins from E.W., get in. Why aren't you wearing handcuffs? Damn."

Jay
Together Again, Unnaturally
Decisions are easy when you don't have many choices.

I know I hurt Gabs badly. I chose land, not family. That's a sin to a MacBride. I swear to God I'd have done whatever it took to make it up to her. She wasn't ready to trust me then, and I couldn't undo my decisions now. I had to be the kind of man she wouldn't trust just a little while longer. Until E.W. stuck his head too far into the trap to back out.

I could only hope the end results would justify the means.

And conversations are hard when one of us isn't talking.

We were roaring into the mountains above Asheville, and Gabs hadn't said one word yet. The last time I'd seen her, she'd stared at me with eyes that had gone so black I couldn't see the green irises at all; a blue vein had throbbed in her cheek, where the skin looked translucent. The freckles across her nose had turned into reverse stars. Her long red hair seemed to catch fire. She told me I was doomed. Then she walked out.

"I didn't have you arrested," I said above the grim silence. "The handcuffs remark was just a personal fantasy."

Not a peep in response.

I turned up the heater. The cab was dark and cozy-warm. I had music on standby, if she'd say the word. "Ask me anything you want," I said. "I'll leave out pieces of the entire truth, but I won't lie to you directly."

I heard the agitated rush of her breathing as she finished mentally nailing all of her doors shut and pushing furniture in front of them. I let her build her barricades.

"What will happen to those kids? You're after Dustin, too, aren't you?" she asked. "Charlie told me they're all under E.W.'s guardianship."

"If I can get them to trust me? Nothing. Or at least not Straithern."

"Would he send both of the boys to Straithern?"

I winced. She knew about my years there. I'd never told her; she'd done the research. "He'd send Dustin. Donny doesn't even qualify as ring bait."

"Ring bait?"

"The puppies they throw in the cages with pit bulls to teach them to kill."

Silence. She turned her face away from me, set her purse in the floor between her feet, and spread her coat over her legs. "You learned to kill?"

"Metaphorically speaking."

The sound she made was low and quickly cut off by a hand to her throat. The sadness in it went through me. I focused on the dark road for several minutes, forcing the emotion into the back corners of my brain. Getting it under control. "Check out the picnic I brought for you," I said. "In that backpack on the floor."

She rummaged in the canvas pack and pulled out a large jar of cayenne pepper flakes. That's all the bag contained.

We lay together on rumpled sheets in a room overlooking the Malibu surf. She held up the tin of hot pepper flakes and dangled it just above my thighs. "This is how much I love you. I'll sprinkle it on . . . and lick it off. I can take the sting. Can you?"

I stroked a finger along her cheek and smiled, then she opened the tin . . .

She set the can between us. Was that a come-hither hint or a dream-on-you-bastard, gesture? A man can hope. A Wakefield faces reality. Her answer? *Dream on.*

"What makes you think E.W. won't send people to look for the kids up here?"

I took a long drag on the cigar. "He doesn't have to. He knows I'm going to bring them back."

"So . . . this is a game? These kids are pawns in a chess match between you two?"

"Nothing's a game where we're concerned. It's a war."

"It's my war, too, Jay. I have good reason to hate E.W. And I'd like to see this fabled

138

Little Finn."

"Good. I thought you'd want a piece of the action. In fact, I'm hoping you'll be my ambassador. A *fabled* MacBride."

"The old moonshining stories? That's not my family."

"Can't be sure."

"Why would the people up in the Little Finn Valley today possibly care?"

"They're not normal. You'll see. You're a MacBride, and that name carries a lot of weight in this part of the mountains, whether you realize it or not. Especially at Fortress Du Bonavendier, for reasons I don't completely understand. It's partly because an ancestor of yours was also a Nettie, which means a lot up there. You're my trading card. If I come bearing a Mac-Bride, I'm halfway to being a trusted ally."

She hissed. *Hissed.* I was glad they took away her Taser at the police station.

The soft, squeaking compression of her body shoving backward into the seat's deep fleece-and-leather back told me she was on guard and unlikely to segue into a better mood. My stomach, already in a cold knot of disgust at how my relatively simple plan had already gone to hell, tightened more. I was counting on her to up my cred with the general populace. E.W. had to believe I was

coming off this mountain with the kids. And
Dustin. His spy had to tell him I could pull
this off, win their trust and deliver his heir
in exchange for the mining rights. I had to
prove he cashed his blood like poker chips.
I had to dirty the man so well that he'd
never get clean in the public eye.

I needed proof he was capable of trading
his own blood for money. E.W. was about
to hand it to me on a silver platter.

She lifted her hands to her mane of damp
red hair, which she'd shoved into a tortoise-
shell clip as we left the police station. She
re-secured the mass by pushing and twisting its long strands into a tight knot.

"Getting ready for battle?"

"Yep. If I get waterboarded tonight because I've helped with your scheme to screw
E.W., it will frizz."

A strange thing happened. I laughed. She
was the only woman who could pull real joy
out of me, even for just a second. I loved
being with her again.

Time for the test. I handed her my cigar.
Would she remember what she'd done with
a similar one within the first thirty minutes
of our doomed reunion, thirteen years ago?

She took the fat, damp, phallic offering
between her thumb and forefinger, sneering
as if it were a stinking, rotten cucumber

even her briny magic couldn't save. Then she lowered her window. She heaved the very expensive, hand-rolled smoke into the soggy mountain night.

Yep, she remembered. I laughed again. "You MacBrides are a hard people."

Gabby
Into the Valley of the Shadow of Wakefield

Two hours northeast of Asheville, we entered the isolated heart of the Carolina Appalachians. Most of the territory is held in national and state forest, with only pockets of private land left. There were miles of dark hollows and unexplored ridges, hidden places brimming with unfound troves of history, the archaeology of forgotten Cherokee villages and the overgrown foundations of tiny pioneer cabins where people lived their entire lives without being recorded in any civic ledger. Some of them still did.

The 1996 Olympic bomber, Eric Rudolph, hid out in these mountains for months before the FBI caught him. And then only because they got a tip. *We're in the cradle of a modern pioneer wilderness.*

Jay downshifted the truck as it crawled up ever-steepening two-lanes twisting around the rocky fringes of sheer drops that went down a thousand feet in places, making my ears pop. Occasionally a silver guard rail pretended to protect us from the pavement's rim. My memories of the high Appalachians were postcards, dreamlike. The scent of blue air and a sea of clouds below eye level. Like visiting a world floating above the earth. A kind of heaven. The smell of evergreens and damp, cold waterfalls and the pickled brine of spring rain. Snowflakes sprinkled the windshield. The rhythmic *whump* of the wipers made my thighs warm.

Jay tapped the surface of his phone, and his playlist of our weekend's greatest moments went silent. The deep rumble of the truck's engine filled my ears. It geared down to a thick purr as he shifted again. The two-lane began to descend, and a few minutes later, trees closed in on both sides. We were deep into the mountain's broad, shallow flank.

We're inside the arms of this mountain range now.

Ahead, an opening in the trees yawed off into unknown forests. A thick metal arm blocked the entrance to a narrow gravel lane. "Time to leave reality behind," Jay said, then swung the truck off the public road. We crunched to a halt with the truck's grill almost touching the barricade arm. The arm's right end disappeared into a thick control box with a stone base. The arm whirred upward. We drove past.

The headlights glinted off a device up in a tree. A security camera.

Checkpoint Ahead. Guard On Duty.

"Is this where I throw my bong out the window and hide my guns?" I asked grimly.

"No, this is where you lock and load."

"The bong, or the guns?"

"Both."

A light winked through the bare winter forest. We crossed a wide stone bridge that surprised me with its vintage look — it seemed very old, as if the road had been built to reach it. Another curve came and went, then the road opened into a broad glen with a parking area in front of several log and stone buildings. There was a loading dock, a bulletin board under a porch, rocking chairs, planters bursting with hardy evergreen shrubs, old trucks, a goose-necked horse trailer . . . and several free-range buffalo. They stood around a sheltered feeding kiosk, pulling shanks of hay from a tall wire cage, chewing placidly. Mildly interested, the bull of the small clan lifted his shaggy head and watched us. The cows didn't even bother to pretend they noticed.

The buildings looked just as entrenched. Each had tall, barred windows across the fronts, but their back halves disappeared into the side of a hill. The roofs were flat and sodded. A snug little log shed stood atop the largest building. Security lights came on, filling our cab with antiseptic light. Squinting, I saw a radio tower reaching high above the tree tops, and I also saw five goats. They gazed out at us from the roof, standing in the rooftop shed's doorway. They looked warm and happy, standing in a deep bed of hay.

On the roof. Goats on the roof.

"Goat Central," Jay said. "Will's father built it in the seventies. Jack Bonavendier. The locals come here for help in emergencies. Groceries. Propane. Medicine. Clothes for their kids. Any kind of emergency aid that they can't afford or are too proud — or too skittish — to apply for from the government. Jack Bonavendier was the reason this forgotten community survived. Will is the reason it thrives." He paused, as if redefining Will's generosity. "Welfare for the lazy and uneducated. He builds loyalty with handouts."

"Or through kindness to those who are isolated and forgotten by the mainstream."

"Bleeding heart."

"Elitist Ayn Rand toady."

"Naïve bunny kisser."

144

"Right-wing capitalist."

"Foodie socialist."

"Corporate apologist."

"Artsy dreamer."

I reached for my door latch. The buffalo looked safe to me. I pictured them as steaks soaking in a pickly marinade. "I need some air."

Click.

My door lock went down. I turned slowly to stare at Jay. "Nothing personal," he said. "It's not safe."

"The buffalo are dangerous?"

"No, but the gorilla might be."

A thick *thump* imprinted the truck's roof. I sank back as a dark face peered over the windshield at us.

Call it an unfortunate girly instinct, but I leapt toward Jay with my own display of primate behavior, turning sideways and wrapping my arms around his neck as if he were an oak and I might climb him. The instant warmth and strength surged between us. His body felt wonderful against mine. He quickly wrapped his right around me and pulled me closer.

I was staring at the upside-down gorilla face above us. Jay was looking at me. His breath, slow and careful, caressed my bare neck above my coat. "I used to look at the covers of Dad's John Carter of Mars books," he said quietly, his voice deep and luscious in my ear. "All those . . . bodacious women. They were always clinging to Carter, just like this. When I was a kid I spent a lot of time trying to imagine *exactly* how that would feel. To be having adventures on another planet, in terrible danger, with the most exotic woman in the universe pressing herself against me for protection. How incredibly exciting that must be." He paused. "Now I know."

Turning my face towards his so slowly that each breath skated on a fraction of movement, I looked into his eyes and tried not to fall apart. It was the same as that time in California. All the tension, the unanswered questions, the awkwardness and anger and memories and heartache, all falling aside simply because we were this close, and suddenly lost in each other's spell.

Our chaperone began to slap the windshield with the palm of her hand. Hard. When that didn't break our concentration, the hand disappeared then reappeared on Jay's side, attached to a long, thick, furry arm that draped downward. The hand gripped his door latch and began jerking. Hard. The truck rocked.

That did it. I pulled back, he let me go,

but we both managed to trail our hands across a lot of territory on the way. I slid back to my own side of the seat and smoothed my coat. The dark face and deep-set eyes of our visitor craned downward beside Jay's window. Dark gorilla lips pursed at him, then pressed against the glass.

"I'm no Jane Goodall," I said, "But I believe that's a gorilla, and she's hitting on you."

"She likes me." Jay hit a button and his window purred downward. Prying the lid off a cooler, he reached inside and retrieved a cookie. "Here, Sheba."

Sheba reached a huge hand inside and snared the cookie. Holding it carefully, she climbed down and lumbered across the yard, disappearing through a doorway into a barn-like shed.

Jay smiled. "Will keeps as many of the exotic animals as possible. If they can live here without being much of a threat to everyone else, they stay."

"Define 'much of a threat.' "

"The giraffes kick. The monkeys steal and bite. The kangaroos can rip a person up with their hind claws. They travel in gangs. Like politicians."

"How many kangaroos *are* there?"

"No one's sure anymore. Same as the

buffalo. The Little Finn Company owns forty square miles of land here. Plenty of room to breed and roam."

Forty square miles.

Jay lifted a finger to his lips. He nodded toward a small building, where smoke curled from a tall chimney. A light came on. A tall, wide-shouldered young man let a pack of dogs out. Mostly pit bulls, but also some herding dogs: big shaggy black Belgian shepherds and brindled Australian Cattle Dogs, bred from dingoes. The guard stepped onto the shallow porch. Following him was a short wraith, also draped in some kind of hood and poncho, and carrying a small satchel of some kind. Some kind of animal sat atop her right shoulder. A weasel? A monkey? Maybe a pet dragon.

"It's the Clagg," Jay said, and hung an arm out the truck's window. "Clagg Sullivan. Used to work for a drug ring up in Memphis. He's clean now."

"Who's his shadow?"

"I don't know yet. There are new refugees here every time I visit."

Refugees?

His face hooded, a shaggy poncho swinging around his swaggering legs, the Clagg strode toward us. A rifle was slung by a strap over his shoulder. Ahead of him trotted the pit bills and cattle dogs and shaggy shepherds, their heads lowered in that way that said they'd charge if he gave the word. The wraith broke into a trot to keep up. Her shadowy pet curled a long tail around her forearm.

The Clagg lifted a flashlight and beamed it into the already well-lit truck, illuminating his own face, too. He was young but rough, with scars across his black eyebrows and the bridge of his nose. Instantly he recognized Jay, and did not look happy to see him; then shifted his gaze to me. His eyes darkened. The hood slid back to reveal a shaved head with matching flame tattoos on either side of his skull. A guttural sound that might be a welcome rumbled from his throat. He touched an earpiece. "She's here, Mr. B."

A tingle flashed up my spine at those words. I sounded important to Mr. B. That worried me.

The wraith peered around him, still in the shadows.

Jay nodded at her. "You have an assistant now?"

"I am a registered nurse," the wraith answered for itself, its voice feminine and lightly accented. "I work for Doctor Fortunato." She stepped from the shadows, revealing a round face with dark eyes and olive skin. Black bangs shagged over her forehead. "My name is Woserit Elmessiri. But please refer to me as 'Wren.' " She craned her head and gazed at me with the same intense curiosity as Clagg.

"Wren's an Arab," Clagg added matter-of-factly. "Don't be scared, she's not Muslim. She's from Egypt, and she's a Jesus freak."

Wren frowned at him.

"And the rat on her shoulder doesn't bite. So don't freak out."

"It's a kudamundi," Wren said staunchly. "In essence, a South American raccoon."

The Clagg shrugged. "She needs a ride down to the valley."

Jay nodded.

The Clagg shined his flashlight at me again. Both he and the kudamundi-wearing Egyptian nurse studied me. "A MacBride," Wren said in her soft accent. As if they'd never seen one before. As if I was the most exotic of the exotic beasts that roamed this wild outpost.

Blood Might Talk, but in Its Own Sweet Time

"Look. Eco-friendly Christmas decorations," Jay inserted, making the distraction sound convenient and sharp. He down-shifted as we entered a long slope beside a craggy wall of ancient bedrock. A fairytale tableaux of tiny icicles hung from every edge and crevice. It was beautiful and oddly heartbreaking.

From the back seat, Wren said, "The grace of God's beauty will always find a way through the hardest surface. This valley shimmers with the hope of forgiveness."

Jay
Which Way Do You Turn When You're Already in Too Deep?

"A MacBride."

I hadn't expected that worshipful reaction the moment two Little Finnians laid eyes on Gabs. Honestly, I thought the whole MacBride connection up here was just a routine dose of the mountain nostalgia — the "hoodoo" that's a mix of half-forgotten history, tall tales, and the glorification of some mythical time when Scots-Irish set-tlers and Cherokees lived in some fantasy land alongside good-hearted moonshiners, buxom pioneer women who birthed babies while grinding the corn crop with their knit-ting needles, and so forth. All standing proudly against redcoats, Yankees, city slick-ers, revenuers and now, mining companies.

My cell phone vibrated. I pulled it from my jacket as I drove.

You were right about her. She's the spy.

I drove slower, sorting my options. E.W. had his informant here. I had mine. Did that make us even? I hoped so. I could take E.W. this time. Even with his crazy daughter Denoto on his side as his spy. How she could hate the man and still spy for him to win his approval was beyond me, but she did. I could only guess she knew her bipolar illness would forever create a problem with her challenging E.W. for Dustin. All she could do was play both sides. Be a place Dustin could run to and also be someone E.W. might let back into his life if Dustin chose him. Denoto was walking a very fine line. And I had to hope she could hold it together long enough to do what I counted on her to do — report my every move to E.W. so he'd be comfortable enough to gloat. When E.W. gloated, he didn't remember to watch his words. I could get him on record. If everything went right in the Little Finn.

If.

The road down into the valley went through fifteen slow miles of forest, creeks, overhanging vines and glimpses of small pastures and fields. By the time I reached the valley floor, I felt a little lost, a little found. The Little Finn River was small by Mississippi and Nile standards, shallow in most places, but it curled through the valley's long, oval bowl like a white-capped artery pumping life into a hidden heart. Thousands of years of human history had been nurtured by it. We drove across it on a long stone bridge with steel columns in case the river turned ugly in a flood.

"I've read about the distillery," Gabs said. "This bridge can hold a tractor-trailer full of liquor."

"It's grown a lot under Will's management. He's shipping a thousand bottles of whiskey a month. Winning awards. I give him credit."

From the back seat, Wren said, "It is the very best corn whiskey in the entire South."

Spock the kudamundi made a chittery noise, as if agreeing.

"Stop," Gabs said. "I need to get my bearings. For some reason, it's really important to me to know exactly where I am. What does that road sign mean?"

The effect had hit her, too.

I braked the truck beside a tall rock pillar with a Celtic infinity symbol carved in the top stone. A shadowy lane curled out of the hills to our left, merging, disappearing like a deflated vein, into our modern gravel road. "This is where the old Ballybeg Road begins," I said. "That stone monument marked the entrance to the valley. According to the old records there was a house right here and, by the nineteen twenties, a little gas station with glass-topped pumps and a garage. You can't see it in the dark, but about a hundred feet in that direction" — I pointed toward a jumble of naked vines and brush beneath huge hickory trees — "there's a chimney and foundation."

When I glanced back she was staring at me like a prosecutor trying to decipher the defendant's tactics. "That rutted trail was once a road?"

"Hmmm. A good one. It used to connect the Asheville Trace to the town here. Came through the gap at Crossroads Cove, which is east of here in the Ten Sisters. These mountains are the Eerie Gals. To the west are the Derry Fogs." I'm not known for being Mr. Tour Guide, but since I had her attention and she wasn't sniping at me for once, I tried. "Their names are Anglo corruptions of the Irish words for two mountain ranges in Donegal."

Beneath a solar-powered lamp next to the moss-flecked pillar, a wooden sign pointed us forward.

The Gallagher Center
Ballybeg
Little Finn Distillery
The Memory Oak Cemetery

In the back seat, Wren leaned forward. "Can you hear the Christmas drums?"

We lowered our windows. A few snowflakes wafted into the truck along with the distant rhythm of a drum circle. African djembes, bongos, congos, tambourines, Australian didgeridoos, shakers, frog croakers and, giving a holiday ambience to it all, the loud jingle of sleigh bells. All unified in a communal beat that was hypnotic, soothing, and ancient. The percussive vibration drops a magnet inside your body and pulls you like a puppet.

"I like it," Gabs said. "It's tribal. I think I hear an Irish bodhran in the mix."

I looked at her. "Your dad played one."

After a quiet second she said with soft surprise, "You remember that?"

I nodded. Yes, I remembered. I remembered every detail of my brief, happy time with the MacBride family. Suddenly, the rumble of a different rhythm came toward us.

Out of the darkness roared a dozen motorcycles, their headlights trained on us like spotlights. A half-dozen horse brigade followed closely, along with a galloping pack of dogs — big and medium, mutts and breeds. Some ferocious but most just curious. Not so much a deadly hunting party as a lick-your-face cotillion. As for the humans, their fashion du jour had a Mongolian Hell's Angel vibe: thick gray ponchos made at the valley's looms; fleece-lined coats from the five hundred sheep owned by Anna Shepherd, the valley's maternal spirit and my secret weapon; heavy wool scarfs and fat knitted caps with fleece rims, woolen boot toppers. Also a lot of long hair, piercings and tattoos. True, there were a few ordinary tractor caps and hiking outfits, a few short-hairs with no barbells through their eyebrows, some older teens and a couple of gray hairs. There was a civilized mix of men and women, plus an earthy rainbow of skin colors.

Gabs broke the startled silence. "Are we in an episode of *Game of Thrones*? That can't be Will Bonavendier riding out of the pack."

Unfortunately, it was. A six-foot-five hulk rode toward us. His face was no longer prime lady-bait for *Esquire, Sports Illustrated* and *Rolling Stone* covers. A deep scar staggered down one side, nearly pulling at the corner of his right eye. Black beard stubble covered his jaw. Three feet of long, shaggy, black hair tangled around the fleece collar of a buffalo-hide cape. His horse was a mix of some ordinary breed and a Clydesdale; a tall, muscled, chestnut stomper with hooves as wide as salad plates.

"What are those bags hanging around his neck? Deodorizers?"

"Hoodoo amulets. He believes in the Wakefield curse. He's got Wakefield blood on his great-grandfather Julian's side. You know many people believe a curse was put on my family by an ancestor of yours, right? Sally Nettie? She came from this valley. There was a Cherokee village here, before the Trail of Tears. Do me a favor. Stay here while I greet the warlord and barter for our welcome."

"No."

"Please."

We traded a tense look, but the "Please," worked.

"Maybe."

A bike roared up beside us, and its shaggy-haired rider peered through the back window of the truck. Wren opened the door. They traded whispers.

"I must go," she told us. "I am needed." She climbed on behind the driver with her medical bag in her arms and Spock hooking his long tail around her neck. Off they went.

I opened my door.

"Be careful," Gabs said.

My God, I'd waited years to hear her say something, anything, that admitted even polite concern for me. I looked over my shoulder at her. "Thank you."

She faced forward, her mouth tight.

I rolled my shoulders as I walked through the lightly falling snow. Will's grandmother had been my great aunt Amanda Wakefield, sister to the much hated Augustus and Benjamin. However, Will's Wakefield resemblance ended at being tall, stubborn and athletic, especially since he'd added forty pounds of bodybuilding muscle to his frame. He was far too heavy to play tight end now, but if his leg hadn't been ruined four years ago, in the Cessna crash that killed his father and put the scar on his face, he'd make a terrifying guard.

Will swung down from his charger. Muddy western boots moved apart almost the moment he hit the ground. His legs braced, his dark, pissed-off stare livid, he bore down on me. "Y'all call off that sheriff, now," he ordered. I'd seen international super models melt at the sound of his Cajun drawl, but that charm was long gone. "Timor Vance, he spotted him on the ridge road. Shot out his tires."

"The sheriff's E.W.'s hatchet man, not mine. You're the one hiding underage kids."

"I say we're just hostin' family. My baby cousins come to see their kin."

"Those are *my* cousins. Only yours by a very distant connection. And what the hell is wrong with you, letting Vance run around with a gun shooting at the county sheriff?"

When Will ground his teeth and didn't answer immediately, I understood he hadn't deliberately let Vance do anything. Vance was an army veteran. Two tours of Iraq and one in Afghanistan. Serious PTSD. He was out of control. "This is why you need my help around here, Cousin," I said. *Lay it on thick. E.W.'s spy is watching.* "Because you can't protect your people, your land, your mining rights, or anything else without *me.*"

He came at me with a speed most men with two good legs couldn't muster. It wasn't the first time we'd traded words for fists. I hit him so hard I felt a bone snap in my knuckles. Though I'd stayed in good shape since college ball, I never doubted that Will could kill me with his bare hands. In earlier disagreements, he'd rearranged my face. My reaction surprised me. I rarely got mad, I just got even. But Gabs was with me now.

I was protecting my woman. Or showing off.

He went down on his knees in the snowy mud. Blood poured from his nose. His posse gaped at the sight.

When several men rushed toward me, he flung up a hand, and they halted. He got to his feet, swaying a little as he scrubbed blood onto the back of his hand. Every giant, whey-proteined muscle in his body tensed. He was about to charge at me.

Gabs stepped between us, her hair clip flying off, her red mane poofing around her shoulders and down the back of her deceptively civilized gray coat. Snow and mud splattered her dark slacks and city shoes. Six feet of big-hearted womanhood faced Will.

In her fist she clenched the open jar of pepper. "I was a fan of yours in your Patriot and LSU Tiger years. But make one move and you'll wish you could claw your eyes out of your skull. I'll season you with more cayenne than a pot of five-alarm chili."

Will stared at her in dawning wonder, his fists unfurled by his sides. Her red hair continued to expand in the damp air. Snowflakes settled on it and nearly sizzled. In the stunned silence, someone said, "A

MacBride."

The name echoed through the rest. *Mac-Bride. MacBride. MacBride.* At any moment I expected everyone to kneel. My god, what had I started?

"What do you owe him?" Will asked her, nodding curtly to me.

She tossed her hair. "Nothing."

"How did he get you to come here?"

"He asked me."

"How does he control you?"

"He doesn't."

"How long have you known him?"

"Since we were kids."

"What are you willing to do for him?"

"Keep him from being killed."

"Do you trust him?"

Silence. Then, "That requires a much longer answer."

He weighed all of the above while I stepped in front of Gabs and said, "There's one other thing you need to know, Will. She deserves to be trusted by you and everyone else here. She's the real deal. An honorable person. Oh, and one other thing: I'm not your enemy. But if anyone hurts her, I *will* become your worst nightmare."

A cold gleam entered Will's eyes. "She's a MacBride. That's enough for me." To the others he ordered, "Y'all show 'em to

Anna's house. She'll want to meet one of Caillin's people."

A MacBride had returned to the Little Finn Valley. Such trust. Such faith. And after what I'd seen of the beauty of the Little Finn on the way in, I suddenly understood why their MacBrides must have been such fierce protectors of this place, and that maybe those stories about the moonshine wars were true.

Gabby
Armed and Ready to Season . . .
Led by two women on rumbling motorcycles, we followed the darkness of the old valley road. I put the cayenne away and ignored Jay's amused glances.

We turned off that relatively cosmopolitan path to cross the river at another aged stone pillar. Jay could barely grip the steering wheel with his damaged hand, but he smiled the whole way. He's gotten his wish. We were certainly "in." He flashed his MacBride ticket at them, and all was forgotten, if not forgiven.

At the back edge of broad pastures that spread into winter fields stood a large stone house capped with steep eaves and surrounded by enormous oaks. Not modern in design, it looked like some country manor from the hinterlands of Ireland — except for the solar panels on the roof, the rainwater collection barrels at every downspout, the tall wind turbines turning lazily in the snowy air, and the huge greenhouse a short walk away.

Campfires dotted the yard. Small tents, some not more than lean-tos, rimmed the fires. The men and women, young and old, lounged on fat rugs and sleeping bags in the light snow. They were a mix, from a woman in blond dreadlocks to brown-skinned and ethnic. Behind them were trucks and campers, at least a dozen of them, and the scent of pine logs and meat stews sifted through the opening at the top of my window. Dogs barked. Children in heavy coats and thick caps, laughing and playing, ran alongside us. I waved. They waved back.

The MacBride, I heard them shout, some with accents.

"Peruvian," Jay said, slowing the truck to a crawl. "Most of them are in hiding from Immigration. They have cabins up in the ridges, but tonight they've come down here to get a look at you once the cell phones started the grapevine. The prodigal MacBride."

"Why are there Peruvian families hiding

in this valley?"

"They came to the States on work visas. They're sheep herders. Some of the best in the world. The big sheep ranches sponsor them — mostly out west. But the working conditions can be brutal, and if they complain, they risk being deported. They run away. They come here for help."

"Why here?"

"Word got out. There's a well-established Peruvian village up on Wolfe Ridge, on Eerie Gal." He pointed toward the dark heights. "Will helps them with their legal status. Sponsors them."

We followed a Peruvian up a lighted stone pathway lined with the empty bramble of winter rose bushes. The darkness of the mountains and forest rose around us; the low chuckle of the Little Finn River rode the snowy breeze from beyond the brown winter pastures. Large, bare oak limbs made a bower. Ahead was the stately two-story stone house with thick gray shutters on every window and a simple cedar Christmas wreath on its broad front door. Silver stone glimmered in the landscape lights. A pair of tall gas lamps flickered by the steps to the stone-floored veranda. An old-world place, a kind of small fortress.

This home site, isolated by the river,

seemed to exist separate from all other small worlds the valley encompassed. A dozen dogs darted past our official escort and disappeared around a side path to the low whistle of someone opening a kitchen door. A large modern barn filled the apron of a hill nearby. I glimpsed sheep inside, fat and warm in the soft light channeled by solar panels there, as well. Also a couple of camels.

"What, nothing more exotic than that?" I said. "No dragons?"

I stubbed a toe on a stone beside the path. When I looked down I halted. Spreading out across the lawn on both sides of the path were flat square markers half-hidden by snow. Dozens of them, too many to count quickly. The landscape lights angled across their deeply carved inscriptions. Maira Celine Gallagher, age 92, Died April, 1930. Race O'Donnell Flynn MacBride, age 7, died April, 1930. I left the walkway and studied them.

"What cemetery is this?"

Jay scooped a handful of snow off a stone, then cupped the snow to his swelling knuckles. "Not a cemetery. A memorial. Caillin MacBride put the stones in place when she came back in the nineteen forties." He scowled. "If you believe Caillin's journal, this is where the entire Tearmann community was murdered in a federal moonshine raid that turned into a massacre. Happened when she was a girl. She was the last of *the* MacBrides." He paused. "Until now, apparently."

"And who is the Anna-who-will-want-to-see-me?"

We stopped. The white slush melted and dripped from his hand. Snowflakes softened his black brows and hair. "Anna Shepherd. Her family, in Ireland, took Caillin in as a child. Anna was born and raised thinking of Caillin as her older sister. Anna's the only living person who knew Caillin. I suspect her main purpose will be to tell why you should hate Wakefields. And that the massacre was the fault of the Wakefields. You should hate us — me, for better reasons than that."

I sucked in cold, snow-tempered air. "I've never *hated* you."

He leaned toward me, sliding his injured hand up my arm, a hot touch even through my coat. I didn't, wouldn't, back away. "Gabs," he said hoarsely.

"Is there a problem?" the Peruvian called.

We didn't jump apart, but a second later no one was touching, leaning or looking, and we'd turned toward the house again. As we climbed the veranda the front door swung open. In a billow of Falstaffian smoke, waving a cigar in one thick hand and a tumbler of golden liquid in the other, Santa stepped out. His fleece-rimmed red cap was askew, his pants were blue jeans, and his red Santa coat hung open to reveal a Jerry Garcia t-shirt, faded. He plugged the cigar into his white-bearded face and, from around pink stoner lips, flashed me a smile.

"Ho ho har," he intoned blearily. "I'm Joe Whittlespoon. Call me Santa. My gawd, Gabby Greta, you look like your bodacious baby sister. In pictures Dr. Doug emailed to my sister-in-law Delta. Before Delta threw me out of New York. Bummer. Being thrown out. Not your picture. You're deeee-lightful. Mow wamma bow wow. Hello, Jay. Damn sorry about the fact you're a Wakefield. You know you're going to hell, right? Join the club."

"Lifetime member," Jay said, clasping his outstretched hand.

Santa Joe roared with laughter and staggered a little.

I had heard the legend of Delta's nefarious brother-in-law. In fact, last week Tal had filled me in on his latest news. He'd been kicked out of New York by Delta and her husband, his brother Pike Whittlespoon, sheriff of the Cove's Jefferson County, after an incident in Times Square. It involved Joe's naked hairy torso, large jolly paunch, tighty whities, and a sign that he'd labeled, Naked Santa. He was posing next to the ubiquitous "Naked Cowboy," which was now a licensed tourist franchise. Naked Santa was not. By the time the police arrested him on a drunk and disorderly charge, Joe had collected two hundred dollars in tips — the cash was stuffed in the tops of his briefs — and he'd posed for dozens of photos.

Pike and Delta made him donate the money to charity, and the charges were dropped. The *Skillet Stars* producers — Delta was there to complete the final rounds of their cooking competition — were not pleased.

"Ever'body's pissed at me," Santa Joe said sadly. His ruddy face brightened. "Except your sis. She sent me a box of biscuits and cupcakes." He clamped a hand on Jay's shoulder, an effort which required Santa Joe to reach up. He lost his balance. Jay wound an arm through his and held him up. "Good man! Even for a Wakefield!"

"Joseph!"

A solemn woman barked his name. She

168

stepped into the doorway behind him. Skeins of silver-gray yarn draped from her neck and over one arm. In one hand she held a fat braid of roving — wool that had been washed, combed and organized into thick ropes for spinning. Her hair matched the silver of the yarn, and small tufts of escaped wool feathered it. She was lean and stern despite a gold holiday jumper with tiny Christmas ornaments embroidered on the neckline.

"Mrs. Shepherd?" I asked.

She snorted. "Hardly." Her eyes gleamed as they went over me. "You'll do. Got the MacBride red hair and the whole sturdy look. Do you knit or crochet?"

"I . . . no, but my brother does."

"You're a cook? Like your mother's Nettie ancestors?"

"Yes."

"Good enough, then. I'm Nona Nettie Whittlespoon, and you're a cousin to me on your mother's side. I am a cousin to Delta Whittlespoon through the Netties and to Caillin MacBride on her father's side and thus a double cousin to you." She paused as if I'd need only a second to follow all of that before continuing. Her expression soured as she indicated Jay. "And I am related to *him* through a connection in the

Bonavendier-Wakefield branch."

"See our family resemblance?" Jay said drolly.

"Woo hee!" Santa Joe exclaimed. "A fight's already startin'. Come on, Jay, let's us unwelcome horse kissers go out to my camper and listen to some Lynyrd Skynyrd on the CD player. I'll get you a big glass of painkillers. A roll-your-own, too, if you're feeling the need to mellow out."

Jay slanted his eyes at me, something cold growing under the influence of this un-friendly setting. "Do you miss me already?"

"How can I miss you if you won't ever leave?"

The slightest edge of amusement softened his face.

I followed my double-cousin Nona inside the house built by the notorious, mysterious Caillin MacBride — my ancestor, heroic victim, or just an unrelated ghost who shared the same family name?

The Keeper of the Blood

Seated on an upholstered bench before a tall window, with snow falling as a back-ground, eighty-year-old Anna Shepherd did not turn from her spinning wheel as I entered her living room. Even her profile awed me. She was tall, slender, with a mane

170

of snow-white hair artfully pinned up by small combs. Her face was beautiful, her skin ruddy and soft along her jawline, but hardly the skin of most women her age. She was dressed in pale silk pants with wide legs. Over a silver blouse she wore the most incredible lace shawl I'd ever seen in my life. Intricate patterns defied easy description, except for the main motif — a stylized shade tree spread its limbs across her shoulders and down the sides of her arms.

"She's here, Miss Anna," Nona said, then stepped aside.

"Fetch the whiskey, Nona," Anna replied in a light Irish accent, still not looking up from the gossamer yarn feeding into the spool of her wheel. Fire crackled on a large stone hearth; several dogs and cats raised their head curiously from fat couches and chairs upholstered in soft floral prints. The room was cluttered in an enormously appealing way — old lamps, bookcases, thick braided rugs, knickknacks and small tables filled with a porcupine landscape of knitting and crochet needles in a variety of vases. Near Anna's spot, an open trunk brimmed with piles of balled yarn and netting bags of raw gray wool. The spinning wheel made a low whirring sound, like a summer cricket.

I eased several steps closer. She

seemed . . . unreal. "Sit there, on the rose couch, Gabby," Anna said, as her long fingers coaxed tendrils of wool into a perfect stream of twisted yarn. Her hands were weathered, deeply veined, and the only thing about her that showed her age. I lowered myself onto the heavy cushions of a couch that couldn't be modern. Its old springs compressed slowly. I settled into the marshmallow of its comfort.

"Caillin bought that sweet old beast and most of the other major furnishings in this house from the Rich's Department Store down in Atlanta. She had everything trucked up here in large vans. It was nineteen forty-eight, and the few people who had crept back here after the fires of nineteen thirty that wiped out most of the county, well, they could barely remember the glories of the old days, when the MacBrides and their neighbors, the Gallaghers, spread their wealth all over Eire County. Not a single soul in Eire County lived in need then. There were jobs and good pay at the Little Finn Distillery and the woolen mill. There was help for the sick and the unfortunate. All because of the MacBrides and Gallaghers."

Anna removed her slippered foot on the wheel's treadle. As the rotation slowed, she pulled the last handful of wool free from its umbilical cord of new yarn. She stopped the wheel with a touch of one hand, tucked the end of the yarn into a crevice on the spool, then pivoted on her upholstered bench to gaze directly at me with deep green eyes. I was hypnotized.

"Apples?" she asked, smiling slightly, those old eyes boring into me.

I had said "Apples," out loud. "I try to guess a person's favorite food. Sometimes I get lucky."

"I've heard it's more than *lucky*. A bit psychic, are you? You and your sister? It's your Nettie blood. I've heard about Tal's wondrous baking over at the cove. And about your doomed restaurant in California. You specialize in pickling, I know, but you also make jams and jellies. I'd love something made with apples."

"Sweet Hushes." The type of apple came right into my head.

"Yes." Her eyes flashed with pleasure. "An old heirloom variety. Regional. There's a grove of them here."

We went quiet, her gaze so intense that silence seemed necessary. "You must indeed be a descendent of the MacBrides in this valley," she said after a minute or two, and the pronouncement made it seem as if I

173

were beautiful and special and endearing to her. Also, for the first time in my life, my family's name was spoken with an Irish lilt, as if we were old Celtic aristocracy. She went on, "I've spent years studying lineages and asking likely relatives of Caillin's, and of her husband John Bonavendier's, trying to find the scattered remnants of the families. Primarily in the hopes of tracking down Caillin's great-granddaughter. She'd be about your age."

"There are other mystery MacBrides out there somewhere?"

"Caillin hid her only child when she came home from Ireland in nineteen forty-six. Gave her away for safe-keeping. Caillin was wanted by Hoover's FBI as a witness to the nineteen thirty moonshine wars in this valley."

"When you say 'wanted,' you mean . . ."

"Feared. They wanted her silenced."

"She felt so threatened that she hid her identity and gave up her child?"

"Yes. And her daughter disappeared as an adult, and has never been found. We search and celebrate the MacBrides who do come back to us. Family we choose is always so much more precious to us, don't you think?"

Nona returned, rattling small crystal

glasses and a dusty amber bottle on a tray of strange old wood. The bottle was caked with cobwebs. She set the tray down on a table between Anna and me. When Anna nodded and gestured, she lifted the bottle and turned it for my inspection. A very faded label, mildewed and eroded by time, showed the faint outlines of art nouveau curlicues and the words Little Finn River Whiskey.

Nona set the bottle on the wooden tray and disappeared as silently as she'd come.

Anna held out a clump of unspun wool. "You come from a long line of men and women who made some of the finest woven goods in the South. They ran the mill here. You're sure you don't do any needlework?"

"No, but . . . as I said, my brother does. And our daddy was a knitter."

It sounded funny, my big, redheaded father, the policeman, with slender knitting needles and a skein of fine yarn in his large hands. But he'd been good at it. "My brother doesn't want anyone outside the family to know. Especially none of his army buddies."

She smiled. "His secret is safe with me." She held out the wool again.

I took the soft wool from her with both hands, as if I might drop it and do some harm. Her aged but lithe fingers brushed over mine as she drew her hand away.

Caillin loved apples, too.

That was strange — to get a Caillin vibe through Anna. They must have been as close as sisters.

She lifted a walking cane from a discreet spot next to her bench. Its silver knob was a ram's head with curving horns. "That wool is from sheep descended from the flocks that roamed this valley since the eighteen hundreds. When Caillin returned from exile, she built new flocks around their bloodlines. That's a blend of wools from her Blue-faced Leicestors and her Wensleydales. Some say the Wensleydales have coarse fleeces, only fit for rugs and felting. But their wool makes a strong base when blended with the others. Every family needs a core spun from its strongest fibers, tempered only by the finest ideals. Never let a fiber fool you. Look to the core before you trust it for your garment."

I rubbed the soft wool in my hands, let the knowledge come to me, let myself feel everything whispered about the valley and its people. "Candy. Salted caramels. Hard licorice drops. And . . . sugar-cured dried fruits. I *feel* . . . dried apples and wild blackberries."

"And peaches," Anna said. "The Mac-Brides and Gallaghers grew peaches in the low coves near the river. Where the water warms the air. There are vineyards there, now. The grapes are protected by the hills and the heat off the water. Tom Mitternich, from the cove, comes here to advise on the vineyard. In another two years there'll be a harvest of whites and reds."

She poured golden-brown liquid into two small crystal glasses. "This liquor was made by your ancestors. Also Jay's ancestors, through the old connections." Anna handed me a glass. "Ninety-year-old whiskey that's not only worth sipping, but worth celebrating. Aged in barrels made from the memory oaks in this valley. Distilled with water from the Little Finn that comes from the ancient bedrock of these Appalachians, the oldest mountains on Earth. These huge old rocks and the worlds atop them are worth honoring, don't you think? They're sacred."

I nodded and raised my glass, studying the clear, gold-brown beauty of the aged liquor. "How did Caillin die?"

"Died in a plane that went down in the Atlantic. They never found the body. She would be ninety-two this year," Anna said.

"Maybe I should have asked how she lived."

"That is a much better question. She always remembered to protect her own. She didn't let love slip away even though some said she seduced a Bonavendier from his Wakefield wife as revenge for the massacre. She lived life with few regrets, except perhaps that she'd been strong enough to give up her child."

"A MacBride should toast a MacBride. Apparently, there aren't a lot of us left."

She lifted her glass, too. "Indeed."

As the liquor hit my stomach and brain I said, "She liked apples, the same as you. I don't usually get foodie menus off the dead. Hello, Caillin. You must be close by, in spirit. I wish I could have known you."

Anna tipped her glass to mine. "Yes."

The Memory Stones

Where was Jay?

I wandered out into the snowy night, flush with whiskey and profound dilemmas; what to believe? I was stuffed with MacBride history like a martini olive bursting with blue cheese. I stepped onto the front walkway and halted. The campfires and Peruvians had vanished. For a startled second I wondered if I'd imagined the people who'd been here, but the coals of the banked campfires said not. Jay and Santa Joe were nowhere to be seen. And Jay's truck was gone. My heart raced. The air smelled fresh and crisp, like white frosting. Anna's gift, a bulging satchel filled with copies of Caillin's journals, hung across the front of my coat. Her other gift, a beautiful shawl, felt like feathers around my neck.

An inch of snow covered the ground now. Beside me, Nona said, "The memory stones are everywhere. You should walk around and look a bit."

I wandered into the yard, just inside the lamplight of the stone veranda. Using my foot to scrape the snow aside, I read, *Bertrice Dougherty MacBride,* on smooth, cold granite. There were more stones in this section.

Ascindra, daughter of Lucias and Bertrice MacBride. And another one. *Harold, son of Lucias and Bertrice.* I was now on hands and knees, scraping at every stone I felt.

Name, son of . . .

Name, daughter of . . .

Name, daughter of . . .

The image of dead children shook me.

"Seeing the stones for yourself is something, isn't it?" Nona said. "Did you know everyone had been gathered to witness a wedding? Imagine the living souls at that wedding celebration here in this yard, under a starry April sky, with music and finery and joy . . . and then an army of men equipped with tommy guns come down from the ridges, firing into more than a hundred men, women and children in this yard. The bodies falling every which way, the screams."

My ancestors? I gathered the shawl around me.

Nona continued, "The official story is that the evil bootleggers barricaded themselves and refused to surrender. Killing themselves and their families in defiance."

"There's plenty of evidence that's true," Jay said from the shadows.

I turned to search the darkness. Nona stared into it, her face twisting into a tight mask. "Are you spying on us, Mr. *Wakefield*?" she said curtly, and went inside.

"Nice shawl," Jay said.

I squinted and found him. His voice was far too high off the ground for my liquor-soaked perception. How did he get five feet taller? Maybe the vintage liquor had had a touch of absinthe in it, and I was hallucinating. A snowflake landed on my nose, and I scrubbed it off like a kid pawing at a butterfly. "You have interesting timing," I said. "How long have you been watching me?"

"I didn't want to disturb you." He seemed

to rock forward, and a tall gray horse stepped into the light with him atop it. A second horse, darker, shorter, fatter, and looking sleepy, followed from a lead held by Santa Joe, attached to the halter beneath its bridle. Jay had waited in the cold and the snow beyond the memory stones, in the edge of the light. On horseback. "My truck has been impounded by Peruvians on Will's payroll. Without wheels, I can only drag Dustin, Donny and Arwen out of this valley on foot. Which explains why I'm now driving this mustang."

"I didn't know you could ride. I knew you owned a thoroughbred farm down in Florida, but . . ."

"There's lot you don't know about me. Climb on your steed. He's slow and safe."

Unlike you, I thought. "I'd rather walk."

"It's over a mile in the snow."

"To where?"

"To Will. In Tearmann. County seat of old Eire, et cetera."

"Et cetera," Santa Joe drawled. He grinned at me and pointed at the horse he held. "I blew some smoke up his nose. He's mellow. I call him 'Stoned Pony.' "

I'd never ridden a horse in my life.

"Afraid?" Jay asked.

In a word? Terrified. "No."

"Chicken," Santa put in, and clucked at me.

Jay smiled, but his eyes held a challenge.

"There's lots you don't know about *me,*" I replied, and walked toward my stoner ride.

Jay
Over the River and Through the Woods . . .

Gabs looked at home on horseback. Not. But she'd refused to ride in the sleigh which was Santa Joe's transportation to Tearmann.

Ahead of us, in the beam of two battery-powered spotlights, was a sleepy lane that skirted the fields along the river. The spotlights were perched on poles atop Joe's Christmas sleigh — a pair of mules and a wagon full of Christmas presents from Anna to the people in town.

Stoned and singing, "Deck the halls with boughs of *jolly,*" Joe bounced the reins along the fat haunches of the mules, who wore Santa hats. His sleigh was the re-purposed bed of a 1955 Ford truck, *sans* the rest of the truck, painted bright red and mounted on a welded remnant of the original axle, featuring four fat tires with fancy spinner hubs. He sat up front on a wooden bench with part of the truck's original floor bed to rest his feet on. He'd added strings of

Christmas lights, mounds of loose hay as cushions. A lamp swung on a pole at the back of the wagon, serving as a taillight.

"Did you ever visit your mother?" Gabs asked suddenly.

"What brings that to mind?"

"Christmas. Families."

"Once."

"And?"

"My idea of family is different from yours. Families are just names on a chart. Communities are what matter. Don't tell anyone I believe in the greater good. It's our secret."

"I take it you didn't have a cheerful visit with her."

"That's correct."

My mother moved to Europe and married a Spanish businessman when I was five years old. She couldn't take being married to Dad, a Type 1 diabetic who was going downhill fast by the time he reached his early thirties. He'd already lost two toes to nerve damage, and his vision was bad.

My memories of her are not pictures, but emotions: shame, doubt, fear. Mine, not hers. I couldn't say I had forgiven her over the years, but I had made peace with what she'd done.

I saw her in Madrid during a business trip a few years ago, and she hugged me and showed me photographs of her Spanish children and grandchildren. I sat there nodding politely and watching her and wondering who the hell she was. This stranger who had abandoned me, and didn't think it hurt.

Over. Done. Walk it off, Jay, compartmentalize. A human talent I had on a grand scale. Wars and families end. The wounded die or build a shield of scar tissue. Life moves on.

"You do have a family," Gabs said. "You'll always have one, whether you admit it or not."

"I'll take care of my cousins, yes, and . . ."

"Gus. Tal. And me."

When I said nothing else, my throat tight, she turned her face away, giving me some privacy.

I want to hold you, I thought at her. *Desperately. I want to look into your eyes and see me making you feel wonderful. I want to see my soul in your eyes. I want to be part of you and become the man you want me to be. Except that I can't, yet. Not until I make certain E.W. can't harm you again, or anyone else you and I love.*

Tearmann Awaits

"Town ho! Ho, Town. Tell the ho's I'm here!" Santa bellowed. We were freezing. It was near midnight. The mules had traveled

184

as fast as mud trickles uphill. One equals ten, in mule mileage.

If I were a superstitious man, I'd have stayed far away from the cluster of rehabilitated ruins that was once the town of Tearmann. The town must be crawling with Wakefield ghosts who wanted me to join them.

But I wasn't superstitious, so when we climbed a shallow rise and the soft lights of doorways and Christmas-decked lanes glimmered across the river and the snow, I said to Gabs, "Let's just get this out of the way up front: your ancestors built this town. Mine dynamited it. Or they were on hand when yours blew it up. Can we agree that one or the other happened, and that you should keep an open mind?"

"Of course. I've always given you the benefit of the doubt. That's the only reason I'm here."

Santa yelled back to us, "We're here!" He pulled a cell phone from his coat and yelled into it, "Santa Joe is coming to town, kids!" After stuffing the mystery call back in a pocket, he yelled "Haw!" to the mules and they turned left down a path toward a long, low barn and corral. A dozen horses watched us curiously from the open top halves of their doors. Before each stall, saddle trees held their gear. Joe grinned at Gabs over his shoulder. "This is the free public parking deck!"

The rumbling sound of water falling over high rocks carried through the night and added the brisk scent of moisture to the snow smell. It was the song of Tearmann — the reason the town had been built just around the next ridge, in the cusp of a gentle gorge, stacked on difficult hills and gathered like a beehive overlooking a narrow joint in the Little Finn River.

The Mill Falls.

I swung my horse closer to Gabs and Stoned Pony, wanting a better look at her face in the wobbling light of Joe's lantern. Melted snow dripped from the hems of her tailored slacks. Her feet, in the pumps, must be blocks of ice by now. She had a death grip on the saddle horn with one hand. But her dignity was intact. She gazed straight ahead, tilting her head so that a strand of her wild red hair hid her expression. When a breeze came up from the river and pushed the red curl aside, her face was rapt.

She's listening to the falls. She's hooked.

The deep music of the Little Finn was calling a MacBride home.

Gabby
The Magic of the Mills

The only thing missing was a herd of unicorns. As a little girl I'd had gauzy, unforgettable dreams of a fairytale place in the woods where a waterfall tumbled down beautiful rocks into a deep pool where mermaids lived. There had been enormous trees and soft meadows and fairy houses that seemed to hang on the sides of the hills like lanterns draped in the tree limbs.

Tearmann was the real-life version of that dream.

Jay and I stood in the center of a stone bridge across the river, alone in the light of tall stone posts with large lamps on each one. Solar panels powered each one. Their glow was soft. Ahead were two paved roads, diverging from each end of the bridge. They paralleled the river banks to the mills, then up each side of the hills to the houses, and the town. Santa had disappeared in a truck with all his Santa loot, smoke billowing from a fat roll-your-own, like a weed genie. "Wait here, the Welcome Wagon lady will come to get you," he'd said. "Her name's Pug. Short for Puggy."

I looked up the hill at the Mill Falls, a dramatic waterfall at least thirty feet from top to bottom, lit by handsome lampposts, not a sheer drop; instead, a welcoming tumble that wove through large boulders and rocks before rushing along a narrow channel. A finger of the fast water poured into a flume that fed a large water wheel on a large, two-story stone-and-wood building that perched so close to the falls it must catch the spray from them as they splashed down. The namesake mill.

On the hills beyond were small houses and lanes, winding and climbing; the lanes looked so narrow in places they were barely more than walking paths, others were wide enough for the trucks and motorcycles parked outside picket fences and small yards. Eaves winked with Christmas lights. Lamps glowed in windows. Smoke rose from the chimneys of log cabins and stone houses. The different levels were connected by stone or wood stairs, and the areas between the lanes showed where garden plots would be planted in the spring or where flower beds would bloom. Several goats lazed here and there, and a few wild deer. I assumed they were wild. But maybe, pets.

At the top stood a grove of enormous oaks. Through the lace of their snowy branches I saw more lights. The snow clouds cleared a bit, and a half-moon shone through. Moonlight glimmered on a beautiful spire that rose above the treetops.

"That's the heart of the town?" I asked. "Up there?"

"Yes. The heart of the old town."

"The old town?"

"You'll see."

I shoved my hair back and turned my face toward Jay. His expression, in the shadows, looked hard and tired. "How could anyone have been cruel enough to destroy this magical place?"

"Wakefields, you mean. How could Wakefields have been so cruel. Anna has made it clear we are to blame for most every setback the valley has had, yes?"

I stiffened. "No, she mostly just told me not to judge a yarn too quickly. Maybe you should take that to heart, too."

"Okay. If we're going to leave the baggage at the stone, I want you to understand something." His deep voice purred inside me. "The rules here are . . . different."

"*Now* you tell me."

Suddenly a large truck rumbled out of the woods — not down the hill from town — and rushed toward us at high speed, spewing wet snow behind its tires. Jay stepped in front of me. The truck slushed to a stop at the bridge's handsome stone pilings, sliding sideways to reveal, on the open wooden platform of its bed, an enormous wild hog with long tusks. The boar's lifeless head hung off the end of the frayed planks, dark blood clotting around the wide gash in its throat. Another clump of dried blood marked the spot where a bullet had hit its forehead.

"Nice Welcome Wagon," I said. "Where's our complimentary sack of entrails?"

"That is not Pug. That's Denoto. My cousin. I'll explain, later."

"Challenge!" Denoto yelled as she leapt out of her truck. "I challenge you, Jay!"

The dark-haired Valkyrie was my height, but leaner than me — that was obvious even in a padded camo jumpsuit, unfortunately. She stomped toward us on bloody hiking boots, carrying her anger with a bodybuilder's swagger. Obviously, she was cycling manic today. Her mop of brunette hair was pulled back with some kind of fur headband.

Probably made from a human scalp.

"How dare you come here, to our home and try to snatch my son away from me."

"If I don't intercede, E.W. will call it a kidnapping, and this valley will be swarming with men in riot gear. It doesn't help that the sheriff's got four flat tires already."

190

"So you're going to hand Dustin back to that old bastard? Along with Donny and Arwen?"

"You don't beat E.W. by breaking the rules. You beat him by using the rules in ways he doesn't expect. Let's take this one step at a time. Spend Christmas with Dustin. Let Donny and Arwen calm down. Then I'll take them with me — somewhere. Not to E.W. But they can't stay here."

"You'll use them as bargaining chips. Just like you used me and Quincy."

"You're blaming me for tactics E.W. used. I was just another pawn in his system."

She swung towards me. "So you're the fabled MacBride," she said sarcastically. "The little charity case Jay adopted as a pet, all grown up and still looking for hand-outs. You know that property near the Crossroads Cove belongs to your family, don't you? Or should. Or did. But he's never going to give it to you. Not unless you make it worth his while."

The Free Wheeler discussion was . . . complicated and one I'd shied away from, figuring we should cross one bridge at a time. The kids were a good neutral ground. Much safer than a conversation about the old bike factory Tal was head over heels in love with despite the strange old story about

Mr. Sam being our grandfather and Jay wanting us to work there, as he developed the place into some sort of mountain resort. Nothing was ever as simple as it seemed with Jay's offers. And nothing this woman said about him struck me as trustworthy. Her scent rose in my mind. Onions. And then . . . liver. The double whammy of trouble. No, I would not be discussing Free Wheeler with her.

"Nice to meet you, too."

"Shut up." She raised a fist at Jay. "I challenge you. Tomorrow. Noon. At The Rock Ring. You choose the game."

"I'm not getting in the ring with you."

"Coward."

"That's right. You'd hurt me. I'm at a disadvantage." He held up his hands — one with swollen knuckles, the other wrapped in a bandage. "Have mercy," he said drily.

"You're a gutless wonder. A parasitic entity that sucks money out of the system and puts nothing back but pollution and disease and poverty."

"I take exception to *parasitic*. I prefer 'avaricious.' "

"You're not fit to clean Will's bathroom."

"I thought he uses an eco-toilet that cleans itself."

"I challenge you, and you have to accept!"

She lunged towards him, shaking her fist. "If you won't pick a game, I'll pick it for you!"

"Fine. Go ahead. I won't be there."

"Excuse me," I began. "I'll be his proxy."

"No." Jay's face went dark. "No."

Denoto spat on the stones. "Yes, you would step in to protect her. She's so delicate. Like an overfed sow." She leapt forward, shoving my shoulders with her palms. I swayed but didn't stumble. "Challenge!" she taunted.

Jay thrust an arm between us. "Touch her again and I'll stop treating you like a girl."

"Come on, Jay. Protect your piece of redheaded MacBride pie! At least she looks like she likes pie."

Oh, that was it. I'd had enough. I ducked under Jay's arm as she lunged forward to shove me again.

Right hand: block.

Left hand: punch.

Her teeth clicked together when I clipped her jaw. If she'd expected my counterattack she'd have kept her balance. But instead she flailed backwards and fell on her butt. She sat there staring up at me in astonishment. Then she was on her feet and in a fighting stance. "Bring it, Pie," she shouted. "Bring it on!"

"Okay," I said. "It's brung."

I headed for her but Jay swallowed me in a bear hug from behind and lifted me off my feet. Instinctively, I elbowed him in the stomach. He gave a pained grunt but kept on holding me. My elbow came up again. I'd break his rib this time.

What the hell are you doing? He's not the enemy. And you aren't a chubby young girl having to fight every battle alone.

I slowly relaxed. "I'm fine, I'm fine, just set me down."

"Get back in your truck, Denoto," he ordered. *"Now."*

"Let her go!" Denoto yelled. "She owes me a fight."

"Tomorrow at noon," I yelled over Jay's constricting arm. "See you there."

An air horn shrieked. Along the river road came a golf cart at high speed. Or what had once been a regulation golf cart. Now it was a re-tooled mountain-mobile, with oversized tires and a tin awning where the cart roof used to be. Since it was traveling faster than any golf cart I'd ever seen, its re-do must have included a larger electric motor. The driver, illuminated by an overhead light tucked inside a large tin can, was a wide little woman in a pink quilted coat and a yarn cap with ear flaps. She raised the air horn again, shook it at Denoto like a threat, and hit the button.

Pug had arrived.

Denoto stalked back to her truck and her slashed hog and her dogs and her World of Warcraft fantasies, and drove down a lane that disappeared in the woods.

Pug followed her, blowing the air horn angrily. It was like watching a Pomeranian chase a Doberman.

Suddenly I was aware only of my heavy breathing, and Jay's, and the fact that my back and hips were firmly pressed to his front. He loosened his arm and let my feet settle on the stones, but kept a hold around me, just beneath my breasts. I succumbed, at least briefly. He bent his head next to my ear. "I know a lot about your life in California . . ."

"No doubt you spied on me because that's what you Wakefields do."

"Because I care about you, and I wasn't going to fail you again. I kept track of you, so I'd always know if you needed help. And you did. With that idiot business partner of yours."

"If I haven't said it, then, *thank you.* I'll pay you back —"

"I knew you needed help, but I didn't know you'd studied karate. When?"

"When I was with Nick Sieger, the mixed martial arts trainer." My only significant boyfriend. An off-and-on relationship. I'd earned a third-degree black belt in karate. "It was after . . . us. I met him about six months after our weekend."

"You wanted to hit men?"

"Very much. Nick was happy to encourage me."

I turned inside the band of Jay's arm. Now facing him, and still tightly pressed to his chest, I saw grim acceptance of that fact.

"Want to challenge me?" he asked gruffly. "I'll meet you at the Rock Ring. Let you hit me."

"I don't want to hit you."

"Yes, you do. We could get my punishment over with. Call a truce? Start clean?"

My heart sank. "If you're really trying to earn my respect, why don't you just drop the Free Wheeler scheme? Prove you have noble intentions. If Augustus Wakefield really did cheat my grandfather Sam out of that property, all you have to do is give Free Wheeler back to my family. We'd restore it; Tal loves it already, and so does Doug Firth. It would mean a lot to us. Maybe we could even get Gus to retire from the army before his luck runs out. He could open the beer brewery he's always talking about. You could

196

be our partner."

He bent his face close to mine, whispering. "I'd give you Free Wheeler in a heartbeat, no strings attached, if I could. But I can't sell it or give it away because that forfeits the restrictions of my great-grandfather's will. My dad died to protect that property, and I'm the only one powerful enough to keep E.W. from destroying it."

"And just like in the past, it's worth more to you than I am."

"No, it's worth a fortune in mining rights to E.W. And if he ever gets his hands on it, he'll dig it up."

Gabby
Welcome to the Dead Town
E.W. wants Free Wheeler destroyed.

I needed more information before I reported to Tal and Doug. As for Gus, we were keeping him out of the loop. Holidays away from home were hard enough for him. Tomorrow both Tal and I would try to get a call through to his base in Afghanistan. If we couldn't reach him then, we'd try again on Christmas Day.

"I had a *word* with Denoto," Pug Barnsley shouted as she drove us wildly up the lane known as the West Tearmann Road.

"And the *word* was 'Shame on you! Shame shame shame! Where are your manners?' "

My thoughts drowned her out. Her driving style slung me against Jay so often that he gallantly braced an arm behind me — and I was grateful.

Pug's melodic but high-pitched drawl took over again. She was giving me a five-minute overview of the valley's truly impressive self-sufficiency. "The Sunflower Power fields are over thataway — that's where all the big solar panels are — and the hydroelectric plant is back there on the far side of the river . . . everyone who lives in the valley leases their homes from Will for diddly squat in rent; he's a great landlord! We all work at the distillery or doing jobs to keep everything tidy and in-deeee-pendent of The Gov'ment! Farming, carpentry, maintaining the solar and hydropower systems, or working at the wool mill. We generate all the electricity we need, and then some! And most of the food, and the best bourbon in the South!" she shouted, pumping the accelerator with a jogging shoe. Along with her pink jacket she wore thick tights with a sparkly, holiday poinsettia pattern. I judged her to be in her mid-thirties. In human years. In hobbit years, she was about two hundred.

"The mill is for making textiles?" I shouted. As she swung the cart down a lane that paralleled the river, the roar of the waterfall filled our ears.

"What'd you say?" she hollered, flying past the handsome structure then veering madly up the hills toward the pretty bungalows and cabins.

Jay took the excuse to lean closer to my ear and fill in as tour guide. "The first wool mill was built on that site by the MacBrides and Gallaghers, in the eighteen thirties. The fabric that came out of the Little Finn Woolery was sold all over the mountains and as far away as Nashville."

"Until the feds and the Wakefields blew the mill to smithereens during Prohibition, along with everything else!" Pug yelled. She said it in a matter-of-fact, almost jovial way. Just another piece of tourist trivia. I expected pennants that said, "Wakefields are evil" to be for sale in a gift shop.

I arched a brow at Jay. He arched one back. "So they say. There are conflicting stories about that raid."

"Massacre," Pug yelled.

Jay gave up.

At the top of hills, she sped up, if that was even possible. The juiced-up former golf cart came over the rise, and all four wheels left the ground. "Hold on," Jay warned, wrapping his hand in the back of my coat. Pug whooped with glee. When we landed, I bit the tip of my tongue. She slid the cart to a stop. "Ta dah!"

Squinting through teary eyes, I got my first look at the heart of the tiny town my ancestors had founded in the eighteen hundreds; the town Jay's ancestors had played some part in destroying in nineteen thirty, and which Caillin MacBride and her doomed, married lover, John Bonavendier, had begun restoring in the nineteen fifties. Jack Bonavendier had continued the project, basing the construction on notes and drawings Caillin had left when she fled from the murder charges, in nineteen fifty-seven.

I immediately understood why they'd cared so much.

It was like stepping into an Irish village of whitewashed stone and shingled roofs, the shop buildings fronted by deep awnings and rough-hewn benches, flower boxes and brick sidewalks. Everything was situated around a large stone-paved square with an old fountain in its center. The fountain was chipped and cracked, patched in the broken spots but left to look exactly as it was: a damaged but proud monument to What Had Been. Landscape lights illuminated everything, and handsome street lamps cast soft glows on the snowy patina. At the far side, the main street went another hundred feet and ended in front of an overgrown ruin of jumbled stones and, with just enough walls left to support what had once been a majestic steeple. And in fact, still was. The steeple I'd seen from below. "A church?" I asked.

"That's the old county courthouse," Jay said.

"What kind of shops are here?" I asked.

"None," Pug answered. "The buildings are all empty. Man, oh man, we could sell the shit out of our goods in these buildings. Host festivals and let folks tour the mill and shit. It would be great."

"But Will won't let the outside world in," Jay said. "So this place is . . . embalmed. A history museum. An empty tomb."

I looked at him in alarm. "That's a little morbid. And paranoid."

"Ah. You're beginning to see my point."

Pug clucked her tongue and nodded. "I love me some Will B, but he's screwy. Anyhow, that's the ten cent version of the tour, Gabs. Let's go have some holiday cheer." She revved the cart's electric motor — not that it was obvious, since the motor made no noise. But she stomped the accelerator, that was for certain.

We lurched forward, made a hairpin left turn, and plunged down a lane into the darkness of the slope beyond.

The Underworld Known as New Tearmann

Me. A pickling celebrity as well as a legendary MacBride? According to a large chalkboard under the awning at the entrance to the Gallagher Cavern, I was already on the holiday agenda. News traveled fast.

Chapel guitar ensemble
8 p.m. Christmas Eve
Midnight sing-along Christmas Eve, led
by Rev. Bonnie Bee in the Cavern pub

Library closing at 6 p.m. until Dec. 26
Classes resume Dec. 26, 6 — 10 p.m.

Food pantry by appointment only until
8 a.m. Dec. 26

G. MacBride Vs. D. Overfield née
Wakefield at the Rock Ring,
Noon, Christmas Eve

G. MacBride teaching the art of pickling
at 3 p.m. Xmas Eve, in the Cavern
kitchen (assuming she's not seriously hurt
at the Rock Ring event)

"She was serious?" I asked.

"You're not fighting Denoto tomorrow or any other day," Jay said darkly.

I made him promise to keep his fists to himself, to just chat with Will about his insane girlfriend and watched him disappear into the folds of darkness created by solar lamps. Pug and I stood outside the Cavern — yes, Cavern, not Tavern. The stony hillside was dotted with stone-and-wood doors, and even a few windows set in the rock. It looked like a futuristic survival shelter, unlike the gentle whimsy of the Mill Falls bungalows and the abandoned charm of Old Tearmann. New Tearmann was *under* the ridge beyond the old town.

"The caves go all through this area," Pug was telling me, waving ruddy little hands at the craggy entrance outfitted with oh-so-folksy screen doors in front of heavy wooden ones. "This is where Wakefields came in and mined all the feldspar and mica they could find."

"I'm not going into *any* kind of caves," I said, remembering the claustrophobic shed of foster care.

Pug turned to me, suddenly serious. "You know what Tearmann means in Gaelic?"

"Sanctuary."

"*An Tearmann.* Say it like *un-CHAR-mun.*

The Sanctuary. The MacBrides and Gallaghers named the town Sanctuary. 'Cause they came here dirt-poor Scots-Irish from northern Ireland before the Revolutionary War, with their sheep and their copper pot stills, and this wild valley was a god-given dream come true. They made friends with the Cherokees and built farms and made whiskey and wove wool. They found their dream here. It got interrupted, is all."

"How did you end up here?"

"You're looking at a suicidal former Miss North Carolina runner-up from ten years and seventy-five pounds ago. When I ate too many hamburgers and blew my chance at the state title — my mama's dream of me being Miss America — she kicked me out. All I'd been raised to do was pose, smile and look pretty. I did a lot of wandering and a lot of drugs before I heard about this valley from Delta Whittlespoon."

"Delta!"

"Yep, your biscuit witching cousin. My mama of the heart. She was in Asheville with Cathy Mitternich on a shopping trip a few years ago and I was working as a bartender, a waitress, and a street singer . . ." She spread her arms and belted a line from *You Are The Wind Beneath My Wings*. "And they put so much cash in my tip hat that I started crying, and Delta took me by one arm and said, 'You need some love and a biscuit, honey.' And the next thing I knew I was in the Cove, with people who liked me fat and sassy, just the way I am. Reverend Bonnie Bee came through on her way to here and . . .'"

"Reverend Bonnie?"

"Will's baby sister, Bedelia Bonavendier, Reverend Bonnie Bee, she's a Presbyterian and an artist, also an army veteran, and she said, 'Didn't you grow up working in your parent's restaurant in Wilmington?' And I said, 'Yep, that's me, the shrimp and beer princess by the Atlantic,' and Reverend Bonnie said, 'My brother needs somebody to cook for the people who work for him up in the Little Finn Valley, and to run a pub for them.' And I said, 'I can cook some damn fine pub grub, and I know how to manage drunks in a bar, I used to be one,' and so . . . five years later, I'm the manager of Gallagher Cavern Pub. We've got three hundred people living and working here, and there's not a restaurant or a bar within thirty miles of this valley. So they can come here. I make them feel at home. I'm their mama. Their Delta Whittlespoon."

She dragged me over to a map framed next to the chalkboard. Out of the corner of one eye I glimpsed movement on a craggy ledge above the doorway. Several large housecats and a small monkey sat there, watching us. The monkey was wearing a sweater. A red and green Christmas sweater, with a snowman embroidered on the front.

"There's the classrooms. We've got about thirty kids in the valley. This section of rooms are their one-room schoolhouse. See the skylights? Doesn't feel like you're underground, at all! Doc Bolton — he's a retired professor from down at UNGSU in Georgia, he runs it. Adults can sit in, and a lot do. Like for grammar and math and such. Doc brings in lecturers and shows documentaries and such. Last week he had a big audience for his *History of the Caribbean Sea Trade* movie. I suspect some came because they thought it was one of those Johnny Depp pirate movies, but they liked it anyway. And that —" she pointed to a large space — "is the the-a-ter. We show movies there, every night. Folks can watch on their TVs at home but you know, togetherness is important and everyone here is like a big family. Doc picks the flicks on every other night, then I get to pick the other nights." She paused. "He picks movies with subtitles. I pick movies with fart jokes."

I was distracted, watching the monkey scratch one of the cats behind its tabby ears. "Why build so much of New Tearmann underground?"

"Climate controlled, low maintenance, safer."

"No offense, but there's a serious streak of prepper-ism here, right?"

"End of the world Doomsday survivalist stuff? I guess. The history of this place says, 'Don't trust the gov'ment to take care of you.' "

"Or Wakefields. The feud is still so raw."

She nodded. "Over money and liquor and family and murder and revenge and love."

"Love?"

Shrug. "There's always a lost love in stories like this. Come on. You need to see our fun side. Good people. Hanging together. These are folks who had no family until they came here. Including a lot of veterans the gov'ment kicked to the curb. Will's daddy Jack was a Vietnam vet, you know? Really messed him up, by what he did there. Will and Reverend Bonnie couldn't save him. Trying to rescue your parents from their worst devils is hard on kids, you know? Makes 'em either mean or saintly or both."

She pulled open one of the doors, set in

the craggy wall of the mountainside. The monkey leaned over the ledge and chattered at the outpouring of light, warmth and laughter. Pug yelled at him, "Come here, you little long-tailed rat!" and he leapt down to her shoulder. She laughed. "Karaoke at the Cavern pub!" The monkey bared his teeth at me.

I bared mine back.

The strains of Dolly Parton's *I will always love you . . . ewww you, ewww you . . .* drifted out on waves of amplified background music. My head filled with reckless wonder. It was one A.M., my knuckles hurt from punching Denoto's chin, I was giddy from the aftermath of the vintage corn whiskey at Anna's, nervous because of Jay, plus cold, exhausted, and searching for meaning in the midst of this tragic, mystical valley.

"Will you let me cook? I need to relax."

"Cook? Shit, girl, you can make a whole Christmas buffet if you want to. All I've got ready for Christmas Day is ten frozen turkeys and some cans of pumpkin puke. Come on!"

Claustrophobia be damned. There was a kitchen under this mountain. I followed her inside.

Jay
The Battlefield Beneath

I found Will in the cooper's cave, a high-tech carpentry workshop the size of a small warehouse, tucked around a bend in the ridge facing the river. Here his crew built furniture, tools, fence posts and dozens of oak barrels every week for storing and aging the distillery's corn whiskey. Oak was the only acceptable barrel material. Give that mix a year to age and it poured from the barrels as smooth gold — made of heirloom, high-fat corn and wheat Will grew along the fertile plain of the valley floor, just as MacBrides and Gallaghers had done for two hundred years.

Wearing a thin bandage across the bridge of his nose, a sweat-soaked tank top on his massive chest, and a look of disdain on his scarred face, Will slammed a broad hammer into the stave of a future whiskey barrel. The scent of oak and sweat and charred wood filled me like a threat. Nothing covered by cologne, here. Raw manufacturing of wood and testosterone. Inefficient, primitive, but fulfilling.

He glanced to the left, letting me know that Denoto lurked behind a motorized blade sharpener in one cubby of the walls.

She stared at me as she honed a skinning knife.

So much for that man-hug and double-shot of corn whiskey we were about to share. I put my game face back in place. Rev. Bonnie came in, adjusting the earpiece of her phone as she tucked it into a pouch on the belt of her Christmas sweater and tie-dyed red tights. A tall woman, curvy and strong. In some ways, a black-haired sister to Gabs. "You and Gabby are welcome here," she said. "I told Pug to set you up in rooms on the same floor of the Cavern."

I saluted her with my bandaged hand.

She grinned, smoothing a short bob back from her shoulder. "Women in the clergy are used to adulation. Especially in places where there aren't many other women." She had served two tours in the Middle East as a chaplain for the army. She had shrapnel from a roadside bomb in one ankle.

Will looked us over sourly. First his sister, then me, as he bought the hammer down on a band of iron. "You lured Gabby here to show us you can control everyone connected to the history of this valley."

"If you think I control Gabs, you're delusional. Talk to him, Bonnie."

Denoto bounced forward. "She's a war trophy you can show off to E.W. Her and her sister and brother."

I gestured toward Denoto. "Call off your pet panther."

He nodded. "All right." He looked at Denoto. "No fighting with Gabby MacBride. That's an order."

She opened her mouth to protest, but Bonnie cut her off. "If you disagree, I'll convene the council and vote to evict you from this valley."

Denoto jabbed the knife into a sheath on her belt, gave me a look that said she'd like to carve off some pieces of mine that I cherished the most, and strode out of the workshop.

"Thank you." I said. "Now I'm going back to the Cavern and enjoy some fine karaoke while watching my back."

Bonnie stepped forward, her Cajun Bonavendier eyes intrigued. "You think Gabby could have taken Denoto in the ring?"

I didn't hesitate. I believed in my woman, whether she believed in me, or not. "She's a MacBride."

Gabby
In the Cavern's Kitchen
The big commercial kitchen of the Cavern was armed for bear: serving bears three

meals a day that is.

"So, when the zombie apocalypse comes," I quipped to my audience of foodie farmers, "this is where the living will barricade themselves against the brain connoisseurs?"

That earned me a few smiles, but also some somber nods of agreement.

Okay, there were people here who believed in zombies. Or connoisseurs.

The underground kitchen was incredible high-tech storage designed, solid stone walls and skylights overhead, also a tile floor inset with a bright, sky-blue motif. Smooth steel chimneys and stove hoods channeled the smoke of cooking up through the rock hood into the outside mountain air. On the far side of a long prep table, my audience sat, watching me like judges at a taping of *Iron Chef: Cave Carolina*.

Three men, five women — one nursing a baby at the plump breast beneath her hiked-up holiday sweater, with a bright blue and yellow macaw on her shoulder. Farmers. They managed the corn and wheat fields tucked into the valley's bottoms and isolated coves. They also ran the greenhouses that provided tomatoes and other vegetables year-round. Two of the women were the Moon sisters, brunette New Agers and horticultural experts, originally from

South Carolina. They specialized in an heirloom tomato their ancestors had created. The state had erased their town, Morning Glory, from the earth. It, and the historic Moon Tomato fields, were now beneath forty feet of water, in a reservoir.

"We're rebels with a tomato mission," said one, sliding a bowl of fat, red, winter-greenhouse Moons toward me. "This valley is the only place we've found that has the earth magic like our home."

I sliced a 'mater into quarters, then sampled it slowly, like a wine connoisseur. I wouldn't sweet-talk them, I'd speak my truth. The flavors burst on my tongue. Savory herbs and spring onions, buttermilk and cornbread made with stone-ground kernels from heirloom corn, Cherokee and Creek corn, fat and ripe. Bloody Marys and aspic and juicy slices atop perfectly grilled beef burgers. The Moon sisters were the real deal. Tomato queens.

"This is the best tomato I've ever tasted," I said. "And I've pickled the best."

They nodded. Not surprised. "Damn straight," drawled one. "You should taste the summer Mooners, grown out of the ground, not a pot. They're transcendent."

They and the rest of the group studied me avidly as I diced veggies and explained the history of pickling. "You need some bacteria in here," I said, stirring dried cilantro into a small steel cauldron of potatoes, peppers, celery and oil. "Good bacteria requires friendly surfaces like wood. Some of the best cheese is made in wooden vats that host microbes in the cracks. Good cooking is all about the symbiosis of organisms fighting each other for our taste buds."

Sparkle Alvarez, the nursing mom, one of the valley's fruit experts — blueberries, strawberries, and apples among her orchards — whispered to her husband Jevalt, a botanist from Central America, in Spanish.

"What do you mean?" Jevalt translated. "She's practicing her English, but some words are too big."

I grinned at her and explained in fluent Spanish, "A kitchen that's too clean has no soul. No flavor."

Her eyes widened. She smiled. For the next five minutes we chattered back and forth like excited fans at a Luis Miguel concert.

I carried the last pot of potato salad to a walk-in cooler, hoisted it onto a shelf among sides of ham and thawing turkey carcasses, then returned wearily, wiping my bruised hand on the soft linen apron that covered my blouse and slacks. I wiggled my bare toes on the cold stone floor. My soggy pumps lay in a corner beneath a metal prep counter.

Everyone carried stoneware bowls of the finished potato salad in their hands, and we traded gratitudes via the *bon appetit* of kissed fingers to pursed lips. The Tomato Moon sisters pulled me behind them down a tunnel-hallway toward the applause and music of a karaoke machine.

It lived in what Pug called *the Wolf's Den* — a cross between a sports bar, a man cave, a frat-house TV room, and a co-op, family-friendly pajama party. There were dozing dogs, sly cats, a few pet raccoons, small monkeys wearing sweaters, and sleeping children among the sprawled audience for karaoke on a small stage in one corner. Another gaggle gathered near flatscreens showing Christmas concerts, ESPN highlights of fall football games, and *A Christmas Story.*

Ralphie's dreams of gaming Santa for a BB gun was a hit.

There were couches, small tables, recliners and other assorted seating arrangements cobbled from a catch-all collection of furniture. There were a good hundred people in the Den, most of them looking mellow — and when the Moon sisters shoved me out of the hallway the karaoke machine went silent. Eyes turned toward me. I saw a lot of military patches on rugged jackets, a lot of holstered pistols and sheathed hunting knives, and a lot of damp boots drying next to thickly socked feet.

The men were pretty tough-looking, too.

"Greta Garbo MacBride," one of the Moons announced.

Silence. My welcome needed sub-titles.

Behind an ornate, marble-topped bar sat some rough biker types in do-rags and cracked leather lounged on tall stools, and a blond woman in a denim jumper over black leggings mixed drinks and guided tall glasses under beer taps. On the wall behind her was a large framed poster with *Little Finn River Whiskey* in scrolling letters. On one side of it was a sepia photo of a vintage bottle with the caption *1915's Best* beneath it; on the other half of the poster was a modern color photo of an updated whiskey bottle with 2012 beneath it.

Tradition and Pride Endure, a slogan said.

I called out, "Who wants potato salad and pre-Christmas turkey sandwiches on whole wheat with fresh dill relish and sliced mushrooms drizzled with balsamic vinaigrette? Also, pickle-flavored martinis and a blueberry reduction on baked brie with a side of sugar cookies?"

After a startled moment, smiles broke out and hands went up.

One of the do-rags rose like a bandana-wearing African lion, carrying the fresh double of Little Finn whiskey he'd just been handed by Blond Tats. He offered it to me, and smiled. "The nectar of the mountain gods," he said in a Boston accent straight out of Harvard. "Welcome, a great honor. A MacBride has come home."

Jay
A Song for Gabby

Dawn was just three hours away. Christmas Eve was only a few hours old, and the Cavern couldn't shield us from the pit-of-the night mood, emptiness and regrets. The long day had scraped ruts in my throat. My hands hurt, and my attitude was testy; I felt a vise squeezing my temples.

"She's got them eating out of her hand," Pug told me. "And yeah, that's not a metaphor. She's feeding fifty late-nighters like they're baby birds she rescued out of a nest, and they're chirping and asking for more. You *know* the kind of after-midnight crowd that hangs out at the Den. The ones who've got no family to go home to and too many nightmares to fall asleep. And when the holidays come around their shit is stirred up, times ten. She's their holiday mama bird. It's the MacBride effect."

"Food is comfort," I said. "Gabs and her brother and sister understand that. It's that simple."

"Huh," she said, as we walked out of the cold into the warmly-lit alcoves of the Den.

Laughter and applause accompannied a group sing-along of *I Saw Mommy Kissing Santa Claus* as Pug and I rounded a bend in the wall lined with deerskins, old photos of the Little Finn Distillery and the Woolen Mill.

"Holy sing-along, Batman. She's Lawrence Welk without the bubble machine."

Up on the small stage, barefoot, with a mustard-smeared apron over her bedraggled slacks and blouse, her towering height and extraordinary hair filling all the available show space, Gabs waved a glass of whiskey with one hand and led the chorus with a microphone in the other.

Platters of sandwich crumbs and nearly empty stainless serving bowls smeared with the residue of potato salad littered the bar top. Open jars of pickles sat on every mismatched table.

Singing in loud unison, the crowd chorused, *Oh, little town of Teaaaaaarrrr-mannn . . .*

"They're going to wake up in the daylight and hold their heads and regret this," Pug shouted in my ear.

No, they won't, I thought. They'll be in awe of the way Gabs soothed their hunger.

As the last beats of the song faded from the big amps beside each end of the stage, Gabs took a long swallow of Little Finn whiskey and, as if drugged by the essence of her ancestors, found me instantly. She stiffened, shoulders back, chin up. She pointed at me in sly challenge. "That man, right there, can sing like a baritone angel." Everyone turned to stare.

She remembers. I nodded, bowing a little.

Her eyes flared. "He has a *great* singing voice," she continued.

"Sing, Wakefield," someone yelled. People began to clap in rhythm. "Sing, sing, sing."

"You don't have to cave in," Pug said. "I'll break out the tequila and distract them."

"I can handle it." I wound my way through the assorted chairs and mismatched tables, the recliners filled with snuggling couples, the dogs curled up by their humans' feet on sheepskin pads, the aura of communal energy, the spirit of the tribe and the cave. Fire crackled on a hearth, and the scent of

219

the stone and the earth reminded us all of this was real, and eternal, and essential.

The welcome and warning in Gabs's deep green MacBride eyes, tearing me apart with the challenge of our history and the promise of what we still might become.

Gabby
The Song of Our Tragic People

Jay still moved like a quarterback. Graceful and long-legged, the V of his thickening torso riding the powerful gears of his thighs. A long-tailed gray flannel shirt swept around his broad chest and ended just above the bulge in his cargo pants. He clamped his other hand around my wrist. "I need an assistant," he said into the mic, his deep voice resonating off the stone walls. "Stay put." He tugged me closer to him.

"Stay, stay, stay," the crowd chanted.

The real me is dangerous, he'd said.

"What'll ya sing?" asked Toby, the balding karaoke master who ran the music from a console in one corner. Toby peered at Jay over bifocals with sparkling holiday frames. Elton John in a dive bar. Atop his control panel sat a tabby tomcat with frayed ears, watching us through slitted green eyes.

Jay leaned close to him, whispering. I tugged. He tugged back.

Stay, Stay, Stay, the crowd kept chanting.

Toby tapped a keyboard.

The opening strains of *Someday,* from *West Side Story,* soared from the speakers. Violins and cellos, a low wail of melancholy passion.

I froze. My God. Jay pulled me closer, facing him, and raised the mic to his lips. *There's a place for us. A time and place for us . . .*

The chanting stopped as suddenly as it began. He had a deep, wonderful voice, a little Sinatra, a little Southern — Harry Connick, Jr., resonant and soulful. He had sung the same song to me in bed, years ago, in Malibu.

At the end I'd cloned my body to his, crying and almost begging him to hold me, to love me, to take me again. And he had. It had been the most amazing night of my life.

His voice filled me, sank my body into an echo chamber of hot memories, made me remember how much I had loved him.

And how much I always would.

When the song ended there was nothing but foreplay-worthy silence in the crowd. His eyes asked me to forgive him. I tilted my head toward his, hot and teary. *Come to bed, just come to bed with me and don't risk saying another word,* I started to whisper.

"Tell her that E.W. says he'll trade you the mining rights for Free Wheeler if you hand over Dustin and the two younger ones," Denoto said loudly. She stood at the back of the room, black hair tangled around her face, her hands clenched by the sides of her camo pants. "Tell her you told him you accepted that offer."

Suspicion replaced the audience's liquor-lubed awe.

And mine. Jay's eyes went dark.

"It's true," I said under my breath.

"There are circumstances," he said grimly.

I pulled away from him.

He let me go.

Gabby
Marsupials in the Morning Light

I woke in the snow-cleaned morning light of the Cavern's guest rooms, with the copy of Caillin MacBride's journal Anna had loaned me still open on my soft wool blankets. Sunlight filtered dimly through a lightly-curtained window overlooking the valley from my cozy, beehive-like compartment in the caves, where Pug had guided me after the debacle in the pub. She sympathetically handed me a tall glass of Little Finn whiskey and a bag of Cheetos. Both were empty, now. I had cried and read and finally gone to sleep at dawn.

I jerked upright in bed. A small boy sat beside a dog-sized kangaroo in one corner of the small room. The light softly outlined the child and the . . . the giant rat with rabbit haunches, who had, somehow, hopped into my room.

"Hey. Don't be scared, Gabby. I'm just a kid. And this is Wally B. He's a wallaby. Like a little kangaroo. I raised him. He eats grass and turnip greens and hay. Me and Wally B have come here to ask you to help my daddy. Because everyone says you're magic. Like a witch. You have to help him, or else he might die."

Wallaby. There was a wallaby in my room. A large marsupial whose kin originated on the continent of Australia. In essence, a giant Aussie possum. He was nibbling several Cheetos I'd dropped on the stone floor.

The small boy sitting patiently beside him, on a utilitarian wooden chair with a woven seat, had skin the rich color of old oak furniture, with black, gnarled hair and somber eyes as blue as Paul Newman's. He wore a heavy coat over a *Despicable Me* sweatshirt and baggy jeans ending in loosely laced high-topped sneakers. Wally B lifted a Cheeto to his kangaroo-ish face with delicate paws or feet or whatever you called a

Wallaby's food-grabber. He was decked out for Christmas. He wore a sparkly, red-and-green knitted scarf around his neck.

I hugged a barrier of wool blanket to my chest. I had gone to bed fully dressed, drunk and crying. Not a role model for a child. Even a precocious child, with a totem Aussie possum. I had a sad hankering for children of my own. Mine and Jay's. God, forgive me. "Hi. How did you get in?"

"I knocked. And then I rattled the door knob. You forgot to turn the lock. Anyhow, nobody locks many doors around here."

"Who's your dad?"

"Sergeant Vance." He stood and saluted. His eyes were tragic.

Timor Vance. Since Gus had spent all of his adult life in the army, I had a deep affinity for soldiers. I leaned forward. "At ease."

He lowered his saluting hand. "He hears things and sees things in his head. He jumps when the popcorn pops on the campfire. He gets confused sometimes. He's got medals for saving people. But they don't count, not now."

"Where's your mom, sweetie?"

He shook his head. "She left when I was just a baby. When Daddy came home from Afghanistan. She's white. Like you."

"What kind of help do you think your

daddy needs the most?"

"Can you make him remember how to be happy? Everybody says you know what makes people happy when they eat."

"What's your name?"

"Alamonte Louis Worthington Vance."

"What name do you like to be called?"

"Worthy. That's what Dad calls me."

My heart broke. "Where is he, Worthy?"

"He's in the woods talking to God or angels or something. Will you come visit him?"

"Yes. But let me ask some of the people who know him to come with us —"

"No! He sent everybody away. He's in hiding."

Oh my god. "All right, let's go see what we can do for him."

I'm a MacBride. These people are my people. They need me.

I pushed the blankets back and swung my feet to the cool stone floor. As if by magic, during the night my suitcase had appeared on a small dresser nearby. I'd change into something more practical than black city pants and a tear-and-Cheeto-stained white blouse. I grabbed Anna Shepherd's intricate lace shawl off my pillow. Apparently, I'd slept with my face burrowed into its soft, creamy silk.

I wrapped myself in the past. It was marginally less painful than my present.

Jay
An Uneasy Night Becomes a Tense Morning

"Wake up, Wakefield, you ugly bastard."

Must be dreaming that voice. Sounded like Will's drawl, but the endearment was way too endearing by Will's public standards.

I rolled over onto one shoulder and ignored him. Frost on my hair, campfire smoke in my nose, a snow-sprinkled sleeping bag, my mind on Gabby. I'd spent the post-singing hours drinking, walking and not caring where I slept.

Finally, Santa Joe tracked me to the shadows of the distillery building, on a bluff near the river, and set me up for what was left of the night. I dimly recalled sitting beside a fire with him, smoking a joint the size of my thumb, while Joe braised marshmallows and link sausages on the prongs of a pitchfork he'd "borrowed" from the distillery's loading dock. We had enjoyed music from a boom box linked to his iPad collection of the entire works of the Grateful Dead, Bob Seeger, Bob Dylan, and Bob Hope radio routines. Sometime around dawn I guided Santa Joe into his sleeping bag as he slurred the theme song from Hope/Crosby's *The Road to Morocco*. Then I'd crawled into my own bag.

Still thinking of Gabby and the look in her eyes. The disappointment hurt more than the resignation that followed. She kept expecting, hoping for, better. I could not explain my plan in front of the crowd, not with Denoto there, and not with the chance of other spies in the group. I did have a plan, though.

Cold water hit my face.

"Get up," Will said. "Your woman's missing."

Gabby
Into the Kingdom of Gallaghers

I was mud bogging with a ten-year-old and a wallaby at eight A.M. on Christmas Eve.

"Hold on!" Worthy yelled like a stunt-driving pro, steering a four-wheeled all-terrain buggy through the Little Finn's shallows. Water, river sand and pebbles spewed up on both sides. The sun was pink-gold and bright in a blue sky. The mountains, rising so close around me, were snow sculptures of misty clouds and glittering shadows. Wally B swayed placidly in the small space behind our sun-weathered seats. I held onto the roll bar with one hand and braced the other on a rusty length of rebar bolted to a three-foot section of two-by-four that substituted for a dashboard.

Worthy calmly gripped the fat leather donut of a small steering wheel — which he was barely tall enough to see past. A fourth-grade Anakin Skywalker. "Splash," he warned, as a wave of icy river water sprayed us. Wally B ducked his head. So did I.

Then, thankfully, we were done. We climbed a sandy embankment and headed for a narrow dirt lane, surrounded by hundreds of sheep and their friends — dozens of white-tailed deer, several buffalo, multiple llamas, alpacas and burros, and about fifty ostriches.

Ostriches. Most were nestled on the snowy ground in what appeared to be large divots they'd scratched out with their pronged feet. Their dark eyes and periscope-necked scrutiny followed us as we rumbled past. I resisted the urge to wave.

We roared upward into the ridges. The valley was a giant bowl with a wide bottom and complex, stair-stepping sides; entire ecosystems could live on those ridges like separate kingdoms. We'd left the Tearmann ridges for the unknown wilderness of this one. "Do these hills have any special names?" I yelled, rocking and holding on.

"They're the Haints," he shouted, shifting expertly as we climbed an offshoot of the trail through forested hummocks and deepening forest. "There's all sorts of murdered ghosts in them! But they're friendly to everybody except Wakefields!"

My God. Even the children know the stories.

Wally B hopped over the low crest of garden fencing behind the seats; suddenly I was wrestling with a wallaby whose intention became clear: to sit in the safety of my blue-jeaned lap.

I gave up. Hugging Wally B to my wool scarves, layered sweaters, and other evidence that I came from Southern California and owned no "cold clothes," I watched in awe as my pint-sized version of Richard Petty downshifted again. We zoomed up and over and around the ridges, coming to a vent in the mountainside and hanging a hard left along a deep fold in the mountain's flank; a loamy gulch that probably turned soggy with the runoff from every rainstorm. Another left and we were deep in the steep folds of the Haints, bouncing on a rutted lane that snaked past an Indiana Jones world of boulders, winter lichen, and mysterious crannies that made dark pathways into evergreen forests of rhododendron and cedars.

Worthy swung the wheel up another tiny path. We followed a narrow fissure over the next ridge. He slowed the vehicle, stretching the toe of his dirty Michael Jordan hightop to reach the brake.

We crested a knoll, and he slowed even more. In my lap, Wally B stopped digging his agile front paws into my jacket. A tall, stacked-stone pillar rose from the naked vines of winter. I stared at the words fading in the carved face of a stone set in its top quarter. *Glen Gallagher.*

Down we went, into a forgotten cove so beautiful I expected spirits, still looking for revenge and justice, to burst out of the rhododendrons and gather around us.

Jay
The Search Is On

It's a Wakefield tradition: Never show weakness or doubt in front of inferiors — which includes employees, stockholders, the general public, and low-ranking angels among the seraphim — basically, anyone who's not a Wakefield.

For the first time in my life I paced anxiously in front of the outside world, cell phone to ear, breath puffing in the cold air as I alerted George to organize helicopters and call NASA about satellite tracking. I was wearing a rut into the banks of the Little Finn, while a dozen of Will's minions prepped for the search to find Gabs.

Will suddenly blocked my way. His long, dark hair was bound in a ragged braid that hung from beneath a fleece-lined cap. The scar on his face looked purple in the cold December sun. Above us, over the Eerie Gals, a flock of bald eagles screamed in the sky. "Our tracker's here. I'm giving her something from Gabby's luggage to scent the dogs."

I put the phone away and turned to study a short, sturdy woman with plaited gray hair, ten hoops in one ear, an inch-wide steel plug in the earlobe of the other, and onyx-black eyes in a golden-brown face. Beadwork and leather strips stained in bright colors decorated her heavy leather coat. Amulets hung from leather thongs around her neck. Her hiking boots, beneath what appeared to be a popular children's show character printed on flannel pajama bottoms over sweatpants, had beaded laces. A pair of big, slack-faced bloodhounds stood beside her, sniffing my air as if I might need to be chased up the nearest tree.

"Tofu jerky, Wind Breaker?" she deadpanned, and held out a wrinkled stick of brown vegetarian not-so-goodness.

" 'Wind Breaker' is the Cherokee name she's given you," Will explained drily.

I'm not hungry," I replied to her. "But thank you, 'She Who Walks With *Dora The Explorer.*' "

She scowled at me.

My phone beeped. I put it to my ear, again. "George?"

"No. Gabby's with Timor Vance and his son at Glen Gallagher," Dustin said. "They're trading recipes." Pause. "I don't care what anyone says about you; I wish you were my dad instead of just my cousin."

Click. My runaway teenage cousin was gone again, that fast.

Gabby
Sometimes, It's as Simple as Spam

During three tours of Afghanistan, Sergeant Timor Vance had been shot twice, lost two toes on his left foot to an IED, saved five of his soldiers and more than twenty civilians from sure death, and been honorably discharged on a medical disability after trying to strangle an officer who had ordered Vance's pet dog killed. He came home to learn that his wife had left him and their son, that his Vietnam-veteran father considered him a loser for marrying a white woman and not finishing college, and that no employer wanted an ex-sarge who had joined the army at nineteen with only one year of community college, and whose only certain job skills were tank maintenance, kicking ass, protecting others, and being a loving dad.

No one had noticed that he'd been mentored as a teenager by a grandmother in Chattanooga, Tennessee, who taught him how to put the soul in soul food, and that he instinctively understood more about the art of southern barbecue — from the dry rubs to the sweet tomato syrups to the spicy vinegar tangs — than most smokehouse masters could learn in a lifetime. All they noticed was the silent anger, the withdrawal and the inability of a tall, dangerous-looking young black man to show them the handsome smile that had won him president of the senior class in his Tennessee high school.

Tim's cocoa-hued face was carved with stress and exhaustion. He looked a lot older than his thirty years, but decidedly more relaxed than when I'd climbed out of the four wheeler two hours ago. If Worthy hadn't been with me, I'm not sure what would have happened. Tim had been so wired that his hands were clumped in permanent fists. After a few heartfelt pleas from Worthy — "But Dad, she can help. She's magic," and a long scary silence, Tim had seemed to relax the tiniest bit and tersely ordered Worthy into the camper, then told me, "I wanted my kid to go to New Tearmann. To stay there. To have Christmas with normal people. Will and the others . . . they'll take care of him."

"So you can kill yourself out here and your body won't be found until after Worthy opens his Christmas presents?"

More of his intense silence gave me an answer. He deflected his unspoken confession with this: "Aren't you worried to be here alone with a big scary veteran who's unstable?"

"My business partner was big, scary, and a movie star, meaning *completely* unstable . . . and I stabbed *him* in the ass with a pickle fork."

He grimaced. His throat worked. He nodded.

My head filled with an image. A familiar can with a pull-top lid, a dark-blue label, and giant yellow lettering. A taste like thick bologna. Spam.

"Spam," I announced. "It's Spam. With . . . onions. No! Pineapple. That's it.

Spam with pineapple. And beans. And spices."

He stared at me. "Who told you to say that?"

"I just know. It's a talent."

"It's true what they say about you."

"I'm special?"

His lips quirked. "Bossy and crazy."

"You've talked to Denoto, I see."

He stepped closer, searching my face. "Why did you say that about canned Spam?"

"That's what you love. More than that, it's what makes you *feel* loved. Spam with pineapple. Why? What does that dish mean to you?"

His handsome, tortured face convulsed as he struggled with emotion. "My mother was Hawaiian. She made a skillet stew. When us and my dad were stationed on the base in Hawaii, that's where she got the recipe. Spam is a big ingredient there. They learned to cook with it during World War II. She'd make this dish with Spam and fresh pineapple and anything she had on hand. The three of us would sit down at the table with this giant dish of 'Spam-apple Chili' to ladle over bowls of rice or noodles. It was the only time I remember my dad looking happy. One of the few times we'd eat together as a family. He was pretty messed up from his years in Vietnam. It took something special to make him come out of himself. To feel something."

I nodded. "Food is memories. Food is what we are, and who we were, and how we show love when we can't put the love into words. When you ate with him, you knew he loved you. Those were the only times you could be sure. Now you've got your own images of war inside you. You haven't been able to figure out a way to set them aside. A way to eat in peace. With your son. But you can re-learn the joy. It's never gone. It's just been hidden too deep for you to taste it."

Tim swayed as if I'd hit him with a wave of invisible energy. Then, slowly, as Worthy ran to him and hugged him around the legs, his fists unfurled. When I asked him if he had any Spam and pineapple in his camper, he hoisted Worthy into his arms. Hugging him, they went to fetch the makings of a new memory.

Now, Worthy slept soundly with Wally B huddled next to him, both of them wrapped in an insulated blanket, their heads pillowed on Tim Vance's camo-panted thigh. Tim sat cross-legged on a tarp and blanket pad next to his campfire, attention focused on the laptop balanced on his free leg. I sat cross-legged beside him, the toes of my hiking boots almost touching the charred wood at the edge of the fire. I stirred a hearty combo of ingredients we'd pieced together from the canned goods in the old camper he and Worthy shared.

Beans, Spam, diced potatoes, jalapeños, crushed tomatoes, and "other" were simmering and merging their essences in a large, cast-iron skillet atop a low grill he'd made from a section of chain-link wire spread over stacks of flat rocks. In the "to be added last" collection, piled between us on the snowy ground, was a bag of raisins, a large chunk of goat cheese from the valley's creamery, two large cans of pineapple chunks, and a blackened iron pot full of long-grained rice, which we'd boiled with some beer. A dark porter. It made me miss my brother even more than usual. Gus cooked rice that way. The porter's burnt, chocolate-hued taste gave the grain a great edge.

Missing him had given me the idea. Now, Gus's face was splashed across the laptop as he demonstrated for Tim.

"Like this, Captain?" Tim said, shifting a hand. He put his forefinger and middle finger to the inner edge of one black eyebrow.

"That's right, that's it, Sergeant," my brother replied. "Tap the edge of your eyebrow while you say, 'I own the feeling.' Trust me, I know it looks stupid."

Tim tapped. "I own the feeling."

"Now say it while you tap the outer corner of your eye."

"I own the feeling."

"Now beneath the eye."

"I own the feeling."

"Now beneath the tip of your nose."

"I own the feeling."

"Now on the tip of your chin."

"I own the feeling."

"Now tap your collarbone."

"I own the feeling."

"Good work, Sarge. Let's do the routine again. Take a deep breath and . . ."

I listened as they repeated another round of the therapeutic ritual. Though the tapping and chanting seemed bizarre, Gus said it was based in neuroscience and he'd seen it help soldiers redirect and release the tension in their bodies — and the terrible images of war locked inside that tension. I was very glad I'd been able to reach Gus in the dead of night at his base in Afghanistan. I loved my big brother dearly, and watching him work with Tim Vance reminded me of how proud I was of him.

Tap, tap, tap. Breathe. I stirred the stew and watched its fragrant essence wisp toward the bright blue morning sky. The Eerie Gals and Derry Fogs towered around us. The glen was large and wound off through sloping forest before vanishing into the consuming trees, mostly oaks. Beautiful, giant oaks. Sunlight came through their bare canopies and dappled the forest floor. I could just make out the remnants of stone walls, the nearly dissolved hulks of vintage farm equipment.

Tim's campfire was centered inside the square of the main house; it must have been large and sprawling, judging by how wide the outline was. The aura of tragedy laid a silver mist over this beautiful spot.

When I turned my head a certain way I heard a waterfall in the hills to our right. A creek, probably a tributary of the Little Finn. This quiet paradise had everything the first Gallaghers would have wanted in a homestead — water, a gentle terrain that would have been easy to clear and cultivate, and what would have seemed like an infinite supply of trees for building barns and fences and homes. All of it blessed by the majesty of these eternal old mountains, wrapping them in protective arms.

At least until the end came. But quality

endures, wasn't that what Anna said? The Little Finn was rebuilding this refuge one misfit at a time, somehow the whole of their community would be so much strong than any one of them. I felt stronger from being there. I felt . . . MacBridish.

"Your brother wants to talk to you," Tim said.

I jerked back to the moment. He pointed to the laptop, a cigarette now glowing between his thumb and forefinger. I inhaled its smoke greedily, recalling a phase in my life, after that weekend with Jay, when I'd smoked a pack a day of unfiltered Camels.

Being around Jay made me want to take up smoking again. And binge eating. And wild, cayenne-spiced sex.

I traded my long-handled spoon to Tim and set the laptop on one knee.

U.S. Army Captain Groucho "Gus" Mac-Bride looked back at me from thousands of miles and several time zones away. His tall self was slumped on the side of his narrow bed in a tiny room lit only by a metal lamp-stand on a night table.

He wore his ancient USC t-shirt and desert camo boxers. Most notably, he wore a soft gray scarf Tal's new friend, Lucy Parmenter, had sent him. My gaze went to one of his muscled forearms. It bore a wide bandage. His bristle of red hair, bleached nearly blond by the Afghani sun, was shaved to the scalp above one ear. I saw what appeared to be a sutured wound. His handsome face looked gaunt to me; his green eyes, too hard. This was not the Gus from a week ago, when both Tal and I had shared pictures with him over our phones. I now asked the questions I'd put aside until we'd gotten Tim sorted out.

"What happened to you?" I asked.

He held up a beautiful wooden thingamajig with a wide wooden collar on one end. "Tell Tal to tell Lucy I'm sending her this. I bartered for it from a woman at a local bazaar. She's a spinner. This is an Afghan version of a drop spindle. Lucy will know what that is. Tell her it's my thank-you for the scarf. Tell her I want more pictures of her. With or without sheep."

I frowned. Tal had warned me that our brother instantly wanted to know more about Lucy, a reclusive fiber artist who lived at a farm near the Crossroads Cove — a farm staffed by women recovering from abuse. Gus didn't know that Lucy seemed hopelessly damaged and far too skittish to appreciate his attention.

But this was not the time to explain that sad fact to my brother, who looked like he needed to believe in the power of love on Christmas Eve even more than the rest of us did. All those tours of duty in the Middle East were finally taking their toll.

"I'll pass the word along to Lucy. Stop avoiding my question, Big Bro. How did you get those injuries?"

"All in a day's work. Don't worry about me. Collateral punishment." His drawl was clipped. He was angry. "What are you doing in North Carolina with Jay?"

Neither Tal nor I had told him what had been going on in our lives for the past couple of weeks. He didn't know both of us were back in home territory. He didn't even know about Doug Firth, Tal's new love. And he didn't know that Delta had told Tal, Doug and me that our history with Jay's family went back much farther than we'd realized.

"Oh, just shooting the breeze, catching up on childhood memories . . ."

"Tell me the facts, Sis. I know a lot more about you and him than you realize."

"We'll be in the camper," Tim announced. He gallantly rose to his feet, picking up both Worthy and Wally B as he straightened, never taking his gaze from me. "For the record, Jay funds a veteran's outreach center in Asheville. Big time. There's a photo of a sergeant on the wall. Vietnam era. Stewart MacBride. Probably no relation to you." He misinterpreted my silence. "Just thought I'd mention it," he said.

With that stunning revelation, gently holding his son and pet wallaby to his camocloth coat, he strode toward the woods.

I released a long breath and struggled to clear my throat, then turned to find Gus still staring back at me sternly, from the screen. I said, "Do tell me more about your inside info on me and Jay."

"After he tracked you down in California, he came to see me, too. We talked about what happened when we were kids, why he disappeared, and what he did to help us. He wasn't asking for credit, he just wanted to set the story straight. He told me about Free Wheeler, and that Sam was Arlo Claptraddle, our grandfather. He said the mining rights are tangled up in E.W.'s control, but access is an issue. There's the land, the access and the property."

"He's going to use his own cousins to get those mineral rights, Gus. Trade them to E.W. He admitted it."

"He'll never mine that property. His dad died there. It's a sacred place. This isn't about greed, Sis. This is about a promise he made to his dad. And to us, in a way."

"He can't sacrifice those kids. It's not right."

"I don't think he's going to. Are you willing to give him a chance? That boy we trusted? He's still there."

"I want to believe in him."

Gus was silent, studying me across thousands of miles. A little smile grew on his lips. "Bossy stout."

I put my hands on my hips. *Bossy stout.* In Gus's terms, that was the spirit-beer that came up whenever I believed something wholeheartedly.

"I do," I said hoarsely. "I love him. Always have."

In the back of my brain, a deep, rhythmic *whir* bored upward to my ears. The whir became a fast popping noise, growing louder every second.

"Gabby," Gus said sharply. "That's a chopper in the background. What's going on?"

My head cleared enough to realize he was right: a helicopter was closing in fast. "You tell *me.* Does Will have a secret air base here? What else do I need to know? Talk fast, Big Bro!"

"Will and Jay are allies. They hide it to confuse E.W."

The chopper crested the treetops in the

distance. In a few more seconds the roar of its blade would drown out conversation. I yelled, "I have to go! I love you! Merry Christmas Eve!" How absurd, ending this world-shaking discussion with a cheery bromide. "You look like hell! I'm sending you another batch of pickles! *Be careful!* Don't re-enlist next spring! Come home! And start a small brewery! The world needs more good beer! You're meant to be a brew-meister, not a soldier, Big Bro! You need to come home before your luck runs —"

"Don't worry about me!" he yelled in return, "Watch your back around [garbled sound] . . ."

"Who? Say that again!" The wind began to lift my hair. I had to lean close to the laptop. *"Who?"*

The chopper was no further than the length of a football field from me. It began to settle toward the glen. Time was up.

"Denoto!" Gus yelled. "She spies for E.W.!"

Jay
The Challenge Is Issued Again

After the first relaxing sight of Gabs — big, safe and beautiful in the snowy sunshine — practicalities set in.

I don't like the looks of that laptop on her

lap. Who is she communicating with? What did Tim tell her?

"Unbelievable," Denoto said from the seat behind me, as Will lowered the copter to the glen's floor. "She's playing *Angry Birds* while everyone in this valley searches for her fat, wandering, ass."

"Keep that trash talk to yourself," Will ordered.

Stark silence carved out a space between the two of them. Then, "Will, I'm just looking out for my son's interests."

"Are you?"

Her chagrined huff echoed through my headset like a low growl. I didn't bother defending Gabby against her snipe attacks. Her twisted mind was worse than ever. I had to get Dustin away from her *and* E.W.

"I agree with you, Denoto," I said through my mic. "I'm seriously questioning why I brought her here. She's more trouble than she's worth."

Denoto pounded the shoulder of my heavy jacket. "Exactly!"

Will angled a cautious stink-eye at me as he maneuvered the copter onto the snowy ground.

I watched Gabs close the laptop. She stood slowly as we climbed out of the copter. Steam rose from the giant skillet in front of her, as if she'd appeared in a cloud of Appalachian hoodoo magic. It came from the delicious-smelling concoction she'd made over the campfire. Her face was set in a curious expression — no, strike that, it was the look a cat gets when "curiosity" is about to turn into a mouse-slaughtering pounce. Fine curls filtered into the air around her face; her long red hair waved like auburn snakes in a chilled gust of wind; it was the only thing moving about her. The rest of her had a deadly, Medusa, stillness.

Someone told her something. I kept looking from her to the laptop. *If not Tim, then she was online with someone, just now.*

She burned me up with a gaze I couldn't decipher. It worried me, but it also brought heat up my spine and through my belly. *Something's changed, and it's in my favor.* Her green stare shifted past me, not at Will, but between us, at Denoto. Her eyes narrowed. I could almost see claws emerging from her fingertips. Not a housecat's talons. A tiger's.

She's talked to Gus. Of course. She asked him for help with Tim. And in the process, he told her some things.

This was going to be interesting.

Gabby
When the Brine Hits the Fan

"I said last night that I accept your challenge," I called to Denoto. "As far as I'm concerned, that acceptance is still valid. The fight is still on."

"I revoked it," Will said ominously.

"I rescind your revocation," Denoto said to him. To me she said, "Bitch."

I arched a brow. "I accept your rescinding of his revocation."

She stepped close to me on the other side of the campfire, sneering at me beneath her warrior-woman mane of black braids. "All right. Noon. The ring."

Jay strode around the fire and stepped right into my personal space, standing beside me shoulder to shoulder, frowning but supportive, towering over me in a way few men did, pulling the breath out of my heart and the willpower out of my mind. Little did he realize what Gus had told me about him — or how that information unleashed a dangerous mood in me. He studied me like an investment portfolio full of mystery stocks. "The fight's not happening. No."

I thrust my chin up at him. "Happening. Yes. The last time I checked, you don't own me. Yet." As harsh as that sounded, I put enough spin on the words to hint that I wanted to be friends. He caught my drift.

A look of such . . . oh, my god, such happiness, filled his eyes. My knees went weak. He shook his head slightly. He knew I'd keep what I knew to myself; not risk disrupting the façade he and Will had built for Denoto. I wasn't certain about his end game, but I knew he had one. I'd help him if I could.

Will stepped off to one side, watching us all with a shuttered expression on his scarred face. He was such a huge guy, both in emotional presence and physical hulk, tragic and angry, and yet I sensed a sweetness in him, a love for . . . what was it? Buried under layers of some unspoken secrets, such pain . . . such hope for . . . *chocolate cupcakes.* He was a cupcake man. I stored the memory for future foodie conjuring. "All right," he grunted. "It's on. Per the rules, the one being challenged gets to pick the style."

"Name your match!" Denoto shouted. "Karate. Tai Kwon Do, Judo, Boxing . . ."

"Pickles." I faced her. *"Pickles."*

She gaped at me, clenching and unclenching fists swathed in fingerless, black-leather gloves. "Cooking pickles — or whatever you do to them — is not a fight style."

"Not cooking them. *Eating* them. I had a chance to inventory the storage room in the Cavern last night. Lots o' pickles in the pantry. So we each get a bowl, weighed out at precisely six pounds of pickles for you, and six pounds for me. One, two, three, go! Whoever eats the most in six minutes, wins. The current world record is five pounds, eleven ounces, won at the World Pickle Eating Championship in twenty-ten by MLE legend Patrick Berolletti." I paused. "Sour pickle division. Not Vinegar Pickle. That's a different sport."

Her mouth worked soundlessly. Then, "What is the MLE?"

"Major League Eating organization. The MLE oversees all professional eating contests."

"You're fucking kidding me."

"No, I'm fucking not."

"You think you can eat more pickles than I can in six minutes?"

"Yes. Without throwing up. You throw up, you lose."

"That's your idea of a challenge?"

"Yes."

She slammed a fist into one palm. "I'll *own* that contest. Deal. See you at noon."

She returned to the helicopter, a black-haired figure in black leather and fleece lining. She gave a bad name to black sheep.

I looked at Will. "You put on a good act."

He tilted his head, the dark, shaggy hair and beard stubble hiding what appeared to be the slightest softening of his craggy face. Studying me with what might be affection, he said, "I see what Jay means about you. Bossy."

Leaving those cryptic words hanging in the winter air, he headed for the copter. I looked up at Jay, encumbered by a sudden wave of blushing. For redheads with pale skin and freckles, outbreaks of emotion are broadcast in freckles-per-inch. He lifted his bruised punching hand. He stroked a warm fingertip along my jaw. I resisted the urge to lean into the palm of his hand.

"Hey," Tim said, behind us. "Sorry to interrupt, but I want to rescue our Spam-apple chili before it burns."

Dropping to my knees, I quickly stirred the hearty mix. As any downhome cook will tell you, the cast-iron skillet is a marvel of culinary dependability. When carefully enameled by layers of black "seasoning," aka baked-on grease, it becomes a work-horse of balanced heat and infused flavor. Cast-iron holds the memory of every meal ever cooked in its arms. It whispers those memories to each new generation.

"Perfect," I announced, lifting a wide wooden spoon to my nose, then delicately sipping some broth off. "It's Spam-alicious."

As I ladled Spam-apple chili into a large plastic container he handed me, Will piloted the helicopter upwards. He and Denoto disappeared over the treetops. Silence descended on the glen again.

"I love this glen," Jay said quietly. "This is the best site in the valley. The slope, the view, the waterfall. I see why the Gallaghers settled in this spot two hundred years ago. I want to learn more about them. They were wiped out along with the MacBrides. *None* of them survived."

Strangely sentimental talk for a man who had no patience for nature lovers and tree huggers. My skin tingled. I stood, cradling the container of chili in my arms. I was sandwiched between him and Tim, both taller than me — an enticing combo — one dark-skinned by birth, the other tanned from climbing mountains he wanted to own. One of them was looking hungrily at my chili. The other was looking hungrily at me.

"I'll take that chili off your hands," Tim said. "You're in training. Save your strength." He cuddled the two-gallon container of Spam-apple chili to his weathered coat and headed for a mud-streaked pickup truck. Over his shoulder he called, "I'm taking this chili to the Cavern. Maybe Worthy and I should move over there. I can cook. Soul food, just like my grandma. Hawaiian something. You think Pug would give me a trial run?"

"I do. This valley is all about second chances. Finding new strength. Rebuilding. Absolutely."

He nodded. "I'll take my chances."

When Vance had gone, Jay lifted his hand to my face again. Traced the ridge of my cheekbone with his thumb. "What did you do to him?"

"I helped him remember the flavor of his heart."

"It's true. The Netties are all food witches, and the MacBrides have a brand of pride that inspires people. Pride and honor."

"And strong stomachs."

"So! A pickle-eating contest against Denota? Really?"

"Why is she spying for E.W., if she hates him?"

"Because she can't help wanting to please him, too. And because she's off her meds, and her mood changes with the breeze. They've tried to help her, around here."

"What do you want her to tell him?"

"That this place is vulnerable. That I'm

trying to antagonize Will, and cause trouble for him; eventually ruin him, buy him out. E.W. wants this valley. Mainly, because I want it."

"Do you want it?"

"No, although I wouldn't mind having a house a here." He nodded at the cove around us. "Right here. But that's personal, not about the things that matter to E.W."

"So Denoto tells him you and Will are at odds, and now I'm here . . . a worrisome MacBride in the mix."

"And for all her claims about protecting Dustin from me, she's going to hand him over, along with Donny and Arwen. She's only worried that I'll get the credit, instead of her."

"You don't intend to hand those kids to your uncle in return for the mining rights to Free Wheeler."

"You sound so sure."

I raised my hands at the sky, the valley, my place there, but mostly at the scent that rose in my mind around him. Chocolate. Not sweet yet, but not bitter, like before. "I'll take my chances."

"I'm going to kiss you now."

I took a deep breath. "I'm in training. I'll eat that traitor-spy under the table."

As soon as those words left my mouth, I

groaned at the connotation. Jay tried to sup-
press his reaction, but his gray eyes crinkled,
and his mouth tightened hopelessly against
a smile. He began to laugh. Such a beautiful, annoying sound, so rare, so irresist-
ible . . .

"You know what I mean. Agggh." He kept
laughing. I shoved him lightly. "You have a
dirty mind."

He nodded, still chuckling. His eyes
gleamed.

"I'll drown that spy in her own brine."

He laughed harder.

"Why didn't you tell me about her? Why
didn't you trust me? Why did I have to learn
so much from my brother instead of from
the man I . . ."

Stop.

I went silent. So did he, silent and serious. Instantly his hands rose to my shoulders. "From the man you . . ."

"You don't get that word from me. You
don't deserve it. You never said the word
yourself. Probably never will. So don't even
ask."

"Then at least show me."

"You show *me.*"

He pulled me to him. We traded the longest, deepest, wettest, most erotic-while-fully-
clothed kiss, a knee-bender, a swaying,

255

clutching, sweet-fire interlude. When we finally pulled back, drugged, sloe-eyed, and breathing heavily, Worthy broke the spell.

"I don't see any mistletoe!" he hollered.

Gabby
Into the Rock Ring of Fiery Spices

Pug and I stood on a plateau high above Tearmann, surrounded by a circle of boulders each as large as houses. A plus-sized Lady Gaga "Born This Way," sweatshirt flounced around her rounded thighs, which were hugged by zebra-striped tights that ended in pink Ugg boots. She was the druid priestess of this Appalachian Stonehenge. Near the ring's Stonehenge realm was parked her "Event support vehicle," a large, snow-spattered RV outfitted with mud bogging tires, a winch and fog lights, a large kitchen, pantry, bump-out grilling berth and fully stocked bar. It was in prep mode for the big pickle-eating match. Two of her assistants were setting out a massive lunch buffet of pork and chicken barbecue and cornbread, baked beans and slaw and pie. A Rhode Island Red rooster and two hens, Pug's mobile mascots, perched atop the roof, fluffing their large auburn wings and pecking at scratch corn the assistants tossed up to them.

The Rock Ring could only be reached by a bumpy ride up a narrow trail that dodged and dipped along the Derry Fog's eastern ridges like a groomer trying to shave the wrinkles on a Shar Pei. When the winter wind angled a certain way, it brought the rumble of many vehicles moving up the trail to join us.

Word had spread. Denoto and I were the valley's midday Christmas Eve entertainment event. The title match. The Thriller in Manila. The Rumble in the Jungle. The Dill in the Hills. The Gherkin in the . . . I was out of rhymes.

Bets were being placed. So far, Denoto was the odds-on favorite. Everyone seemed to think that if this were a Quentin Tarantino movie then she, not I, would star in *Kill Dill*.

Pug spread her short arms wide beneath the robin-egg-blue Christmas Eve sky and the snow-dusted breasts of the mountains. "What a great way to spend Christmas Eve afternoon! Under these spiritual skies, with *Downton Abbey* and *True Blood* and *Justified* downloaded on my computer at the Cavern, and my snotty older sister miserable with her live-in mom-in-law and a cheating husband and lousy teenagers over in the flatlands of Raleigh, still saying I'm the family's fat disappointment — but here I am, with friends and a purpose and a life I love, just like I love this valley and our fearless leader, Will Bonavendier, and I bless the day Delta Whittlespoon steered me thisaway!"

"So you could eventually emcee a pickleeating contest?" I asked.

She looked at me, her eyes glowing. "Don't you get it? What's going on here? Sanctuary! Just like 'Tearmann' means in the Irish. To die for this valley — to fight for a cause that doesn't judge anyone except by the size of his or her heart! That's what we're preserving! This is heaven on earth, as close as that gets!"

"You," I said, "Have been smoking weed with Santa Joe?"

She grinned. "Yes, but I stand by every stoned word I said."

"Do you mean it? I need to know. If this valley were a person, I'd say it's hungry for . . . *nothing.* The sun and water and air. I feel . . . an appetite for flavor, here, but above all else, peacefulness. The seasonings change, but the substance is eternal."

Her eyes filled with tears. She nodded ferociously. "Home. Safe. Food. Warmth. Love. Friendship. Hope. It's all here. All we have to do is protect it. Kingdoms come and go. *Heart* stays."

She threw her arms around my waist and hugged me with her head thumping my chest. I awkwardly patted her shoulder.

She swiveled away from me, gazing at the massive rocks. "If you believe the creationists, the Indians hitched up dinosaurs to move these big ol' rocks up here. If you believe the UFO people, the aliens ferried 'em up here by flying saucer. If you believe the hippies, these sweet old boulders were sucked up here through an energy vortex, like kidney stones through a pecker. If you believe the scientific folks, a glacier left 'em and they just happen to look like somebody pushed 'em into a big circle. As for me? I like not knowing how this place came to be. History oughta be like love, I say. Just enough truth to keep it honest, just enough mystery to keep it exciting."

Which reminded me of Jay. I turned to search between two craggy behemoths for another glimpse of him, pacing, with his phone to his ear. Even dressed in his shabby mountaineer coat, corduroys and scuffed hiking boots, he looked like the captain of a corporation, the admiral of a boardroom. His long legs were graceful and confident; his shoulders, impressively capitalistic. But it was the perfectly imperfect coarseness of his profile that made me want to place kisses down the length of his crooked nose.

You're sinking fast. But there's still so much you don't know about Jay. So many questions. Can you really believe he's not using you as a pawn in this game, too, just because he's got Gus convinced?

"Gallaghers and MacBrides named this place *Caher*," Pug was saying. "That's from the Irish, Anna says. It means 'ringfort.' Stone ringfort. She says ancient ringforts are all over Ireland, thousands of 'em. Maybe for protection, maybe to keep the cattle from roaming too far, but maybe . . ." Pug paused dramatically, hand to Lady Gaga's face on her ample chest, "as homes for fairies and leprechauns and giants and druids and King Arthur's Round Table. That's what I believe!"

Pug snatched me by one hand. "You need to rest your teeth! Only an hour until the opening band!"

"Opening band?" I echoed, as she dragged me toward the RV.

"Just a few rockabilly steel guitar tunes to get people ready for a rumble."

"It's not a rumble. It's six minutes of eating pickles."

"It's a soulful battle between good and evil! Think big, like these mountains!" She shoved me ahead of her. As we reached the

RV I looked back over my shoulder at Jay, who was still deep in conversation with his minions or conscience or inner self. Was I wrong or right about him, or a little of both?

Hard to say which.

Jay
Blood Will Tell

"The time approaches," Anna said in her soft Irish accent, "when only blood can speak to blood." She sat in the center of her SUV's back seat, wrapped in a thick, silver-gray wool shawl and matching cap. A wisp of her silver hair joined the mix around her forehead, as if she had been born in the wool. An Australian cattle dog sat beside her, regarding me with stony china eyes. On the other side was curled a small, curly-wooled Wensleydale ewe, a runt saved from death in lamb-hood by the valley's resident veterinarian.

Most of the residents of the Little Finn Valley — three hundred people — crowded the rock ring, enjoying the guitar concert, the New Age rapping of distillery manager Jamal Little Bird, and the belly dancing of one of the Tomato Moon farming sisters. There was drinking, dancing and miniature goats.

The Finnians sprawled on camp stools

and lawn chairs, or perched on the boulders with blankets around them and beers in hand, or wandered from Pug's mobile lunch buffet with paper plates piled with food. Kids and teens circulated like flies around the perimeter. I looked for any sign of Dustin and the silver fairy twins. A small herd of sheep, llamas and Peruvians made their own encampment nearby. It was a multi-species event.

There were plenty of Santa hats, Christmas scarves, and novelty caps with plastic mistletoe attached. The mood was jovial but intense. Up here in Will's Never Never Land, personal challenges were a way of settling small feuds amicably; a council existed for more cerebral cases, but in the rock ring, the opponents agreed to let fate, luck, skill and more luck decide the judgment. I'd seen ping pong matches here, bloody boxing duels, chess games and fencing bouts. But never a pickle-eating contest, before. And neither, I guessed, had anyone else in the valley.

I watched Anna, vowing quietly to learn more about her. She said it was important to understand all the intricate biological connections between our old families. I was intrigued by her conviction that a great-granddaughter of Caillin MacBride's would, one day, be found, and that the fate of the valley depended on it.

Gabby
It's the Big Dill of the Day . . .
"Showtime," Pug yelled, sticking her head in the RV's door.

"Coming."

Going.

I bent over the commode of the narrow bathroom again, gagging on my finger. I dimly noted the thud of footsteps on the RV's steps. Nothing came out of my throat. Satisfied, I flushed the efficient little toilet, then turned to the sink, cupping fresh water to my mouth, rinsing and spitting.

The bathroom door slammed open. Jay crowded in beside me, pressing me to the sink and walls, his hands rising into my hair, holding my head still as he studied me. His expression was rigid.

Defiance and shame heated my face. "Privacy is a right. It's just for the contest. It's not a symptom."

"This goddamned so-called 'challenge' isn't worth you raking your stomach out to solve your problems."

"It is to me. I have my 'raking' under control. I haven't done it much since childhood."

His fingertips shoved into the hair behind my left ear. I tried to pull away, too late. He bent close, parting the wavy auburn strands. I braced my arms against his chest and craned my head back. "So, you've got a tattoo. What is it? Why hide it?"

"None of your business. Get out." He snagged my fist, his reflexes still sharp enough to turn the score of a game in his team's favor. We arm wrestled, shoving our bodies closer together, thumping the molded walls.

Over his shoulder I saw Pug peering around the doorway, wide-eyed. If we kept brawling we'd give her an even better story to tell everyone. I relaxed my fist inside his fierce grip. His belly pressed tightly to mine. He was hard against me.

Jay pried my wavy hair in various directions as he scrutinized the two simple lines of script in the tattoo. His dark brows flat-lined, and grooves of concentration formed around his mouth. "What the . . ."

He went very still. So did I.

Jayson Wakefield.

I will always love you.

Jay

She Faces a Tough Challenger — and Pickles, Too.

I haven't lost her. She never gave up on me.

I stepped up next to Will, whose entourage included men and women dressed like extras from the mountain districts of *The Hunger Games.* They carried holstered pistols and knives and things covered in skins I hoped weren't human. And they glared at me as if I were a terrorist who needed waterboarding. Or might be a secret gov'ment man here to crack down on their hidden pot plants, unregistered guns and, at the moment, their betting ring. Money was changing hands; odds were being shouted all around.

"You're the bookie?" I said to Santa Joe, who held wads of cash and a notepad.

He grinned around the butt of a cigar. "Don't tell my brother. I hear he's the sheriff over to Jefferson County way. Even if he's up in Chicago for Christmas, pretending to be a Yankee with Tom Mitternich's family."

"I put one million dollars on Greta Garbo MacBride to win." My voice carried in every direction. All conversation stopped. Everyone stared at me. "Okay. Ten thousand?" I shouted.

Joe flattened a beefy hand over a cracked and faded Mick Jagger on his sweat shirt. "Dude, I'd love to accept, but the house can't cover that."

"I'll cover it," Will said.

Joe jotted the pledge on his pad. "Done!" he yelled.

A frenzy of new betting commenced.

Will arched a dark brow. "I hope you lose, just because I want to see you pull the money out of your ass."

"Always bet on redheaded MacBride women. One day we'll find one worth betting on, for *you*."

Clagg Sullivan drawled into a wireless microphone. "Challengers, start your . . . I dunno, start your *stomachs*?" He stood at the center of the strange arena. Shouts, laughter, and applause went up. He pointed a brawny hand at the scowling Denoto and then at Gabs, who looked calm, proud, but a little furtive, as if she feared everyone could see the flush on her cheeks.

I felt the crowd's scrutiny on my face too, and almost heard the thud of Pug's elbow nudging the message into everyone around her.

Denoto raised both fists in a victory V and took her seat behind a long folding table. At the other end, Gabs saluted the audience with a simple wave, then sat down on a folding chair before her own personal pile of pickles. Her red hair, like Denoto's black hair, was pulled back tightly to keep it out of the way.

"Six pounds of pickles in six minutes," Clagg yelled. "We've weighed both piles of pickles and we'll weigh what's left of each pile after the clock stops. If it's close, the winner is the one who ate the most by weight."

A pack of tongue-lolling dogs trotted across the snowy arena, looking up at their owners, who whistled to them to come in from playtime. A group from the valley's drumming circle pounded a lead-up charge on their bongos, Celtic bodhrans, African djembes and Jamaican steels made from the tops of fifty-gallon drums.

Clagg pointed to a timekeeper seated on a fleece-lined blanket and holding a laptop. The woman posed a finger over it and watched him for a signal. He pointed next to Gabs and Denoto. "Ready?"

Gabs nodded. Denoto shrugged, her mouth tight.

Clagg raised a tattooed hand. "Six minutes, six pounds of pickles . . ."

The drumming rose to a crescendo.

"Are you really ready?"

Yes, the crowd roared.

Gabs hitched her chair closer to the table. Denoto gave a grim thumbs-up.

"Eat!"

Denoto dug into her pile of green kosher dills, shoving the fat, pickled cucumbers into her mouth between bared teeth, gnashing them apart and slinging bits of brine and pickle skin flying in her wake. She swallowed three large ones instantly. The technique made men cringe and look away.

Gabs stunned everyone by picking up a knife and methodically slicing all thirty-plus pickles into bite-sized chunks — but never putting one in her mouth.

The drumming picked up volume. People held up smart phones and e-tablets to record the event. I shoved my fists into my pants pockets and concentrated on my legendary Wakefield poker face. *Eat something, Gabs. Stop dicing and eat.*

"Two minute mark!" Clagg announced. "Four to go!"

Gabs finally picked up a small chunk of chopped pickle, inserted it between her lips, and swallowed it without chewing. She picked up another, and then another. Occasionally she washed everything down with a swig of bottled water. Then went right back to eating. I began to relax.

My pickle queen owns this universe.

"Two minutes to go," Clagg yelled.

Denoto had now slammed about half of her pile — fifteen pickles, three pounds of briny cucumber goodness — into her unsuspecting stomach. She'd lost speed and jaw strength, taking longer to tear each pickle apart. Her face began to contort every time she swallowed. Veins bulged in her neck.

Meanwhile, Gabs continued roboting pieces of pickle into her mouth and swallowing them with smooth gulps. Near me a woman said, "My god, it's like watching a snake eat mice."

Gabs's pile of pickle pieces was shrinking rapidly, but it was impossible to tell if she was ahead of Denoto. Her hand-to-mouth rhythm accelerated. Getting a little nervous, I worked the math in my head. *Approximately fifteen chunks per pickle, times thirty pickles, is 450 chunks. Divided by six minutes, she needs to eat about seventy-five chunks per minute. But she didn't start until the third minute, so four into four-fifty is . . . at least 112 chunks per minute. That's almost two chunks per second.*

No way would Gabs clear six pounds of cukes at that rate. She'd only reduced her pile by about half, meaning about three pounds, and Denoto was already well into pound four, by my guess.

"Denoto's face is starting to look greener than the pickles," someone said.

Ah. True. Denoto had a glassy stare. Her cheeks were red, but the skin around her mouth was ashy white, except for the sections smeared with green flecks of pickle skin.

Pug shoved through the crowd and worked her round body between Will and me, craning to get a better view. "Denoto looks like the flag of Italy."

Will coughed and chewed his lower lip. He smiled even less often than I did, but he was fighting a smile now.

"One minute," Clagg yelled.

"She's going into overdrive!" a woman shouted, pointing at Gabs.

Gabs paused, shook out her hands in preparation, then sank both of them into the mound of pickle parts. Shoving entire handfuls into her mouth, she tilted her head back like a sword swallower. Four massive chews. A giant gulp. Two more handfuls. Chew, gulp. Pickle juice dripped off her chin and onto her sweater.

"Fifty-five, fifty-four, fifty-three," the crowd chanted.

Denoto was down to ten pickles but was moving slowly, sometimes missing her mouth and cramming a half-eaten pickle against her chin or jaw. She'd begun to sway a little.

Both she and Gabs had entered the territory of world-champion pickle-eating records. The pro level. The Show. The Super Bowl of kosher dill competitions.

More handfuls went into Gabs's mouth. She was swaying a little herself, and struggling to swallow. But the steely look in her eyes revealed the pure light of pickled defiance. I swear her eyes were turning greener. She had been infused by the pickle spirit.

"Thirty, twenty-nine, twenty-eight."

I began to chant silently. *Eat, eat, eat.*

"She's ahead of Denoto!" Pug shouted. "She's going to hit the Big Six!"

Oh, my God, it was true. Denoto was barely moving, and had five pickles left. But Gabs was moving even faster than before, smashing double clutches of pickle parts into her mouth. Her cheeks bulged like a hamster's. There was no shred of self-conscious vanity. She didn't care what she looked like as long as she got the job done. God, how I loved that about her.

"Ten, nine, eight . . ."

Gabs's pickle pile was down to four, maybe five, palm-sized scoops. She bent low and scraped the entire mound toward her open mouth, mashing a disgusting pulp of squashed pickle innards into her face.

Denoto wobbled, weakly lifting her last pickle to her lips.

"Five, four, three . . ."

Gabs raised her head. Every freakin' piece of every freakin' pickle was now bulging her cheeks out. She stood, chewing, head back.

"Down it, down it, down it!"

"Two, one . . ."

Denoto let the last pickle drop, untouched. Her head sank to the table. She clutched her stomach.

Gabs swallowed the last chew.

"Time's up!"

The crowd roared. A handful of unlucky bettors, including Will, looked glum. People surged toward Gabs, whistling and applauding. She raised her pickle-smeared hands in victory as she turned, searching the crowd. Ignoring her new fame and her new fans, she looked only for me.

Funny, how my knees went weak, knowing that she was.

Gabby
The Spoils Go to the Winner

Yes, I purged my pickles. Jay knew about that, and even stood outside the RV's bathroom holding a wet washcloth for me, as I finished. If I hadn't emptied six pounds of vinegared pickles from my stomach I'd have been too sick, and too bloated, to do more than lay down and moan for the next several days.

As it was, I felt as if I'd had a balloon inflated in my stomach. My jaw hurt from chewing, my back ached from retching, my throat was sore, and adrenaline made me light-headed, on top of feeling scraped raw from the inside out. Jay and Pug shepherded me down the mountain and into a rattling old Ford truck she used for running errands between New Tearmann and the distillery. She draped a quilt around me. Jay tossed my suitcase into the truck's bed.

Santa Joe, decked out in a lei of hundred-dollar bills he'd won from betting on me, appeared from somewhere and said, "Here, it's good for what ails you. You need a bit of dough in your stomach," then handed me a thick piece of bread smeared with butter. "My special-recipe butter. Cathy Deen loves it."

With a wave good-bye from Pug and Santa and nodding at their suggestion we drop in on Dustin who was staying somewhere along the way to our destination, Jay drove across the Little Finn and along its western hills, winding deep between winter fields where wheat and corn would grow in the spring. I ate the hearty bread without asking any questions, getting hungrier and more relaxed with every bite. Somewhere in the back of my dazed brain Jay said, "Take it slow, that butter's loaded," but I was too tired to get the joke.

Deer and sheep moved in herds across my vision. The deer switched their tails at our intrusion, their white undercoat flashing beneath the winter-gray. "They're so graceful," I said in wonder. "They barely touch the snow with their hooves. They're reindeer! They're Santa's deer! They're about to fly, I should go kiss them!"

"Do you remember the time you kissed me outside the walk-in cooler at the PB and S?" Jay asked. "When we were kids?"

I waved my hands dramatically. "No, I remember the time you kissed *me*. You wanted to kiss me, so I gave you an opportunity."

"Do you remember when George Washington led Luke Skywalker and Hans Solo on a mission to save the empire from Darth Vader and the Pirates of the Caribbean?"

"What?"

"Just checking to see how many fantasies you've accepted as truth."

I snorted. "You liked being kissed. *That's*

what I remember."

He laughed. I restrained myself from saying how much I loved the sound. I leaned my forehead against the window and gazed at the herds that wandered this amazing valley. Among the deer and sheep were shaggy bison and, assuming I wasn't just stoned and imagining it, some bovines that looked a whole lot like ordinary brown-and-white milk cows. I tucked Anna's beautiful shawl around my neck. I was traveling through the enchanted land of Oz, with the Wizard at my side, and nothing else mattered.

When Jay guided the old rattletrap of a truck down a dirt lane into a snowy alcove in the mountain side, I gazed out the window at what appeared to be a shingled wood-and-stone fairy cottage among enormous oaks. "Bless your heart," I drawled with a childhood southern twang. "Where'd y'all find this tree house?"

"Gone Southern much?" Jay joked gently.

"Reconnectin' with ma roots."

"Y'all is not singular; it is a universal plural, encompassing friends, neighbors, family, cousins, tribes, and nations. The Greater You All."

"Y'all," I said. "It means 'you and whoever.' Who is the 'whoever?' "

"Anna sent us here."

"Why?"

"John Bonavendier built this cottage for Caillin in the nineteen fifties." Jay reached over and smoothed my tangled hair away from my forehead. "I think Anna believes Caillin has given us her blessing."

"Is Anna secretly on your side, the same as Will?"

He nodded. "I'm not sure why, but she says John and Caillin would have believed in me."

Stunned, I let him guide me up stone steps worn on the edges by decades of rain and weather. Wrapped like a human burrito in the quilt and shawl, I leaned into him when we reached a landing high among the delicately naked branches of the tree canopies. "Some day we'll find out what really happened in this valley." I put a hand to my quilted heart. "Don't you want to know?"

He paused from unlocking an arching wooden door with a key Anna had given him. "I'm not sure. The past can't be changed. I like things right now, the way they are. Between us."

I couldn't disagree with that. I nodded. My eyelids began to feel heavy. "Truce?"

He pulled me to him in a deep hug. I burrowed my face into the crook of his neck. "Truce," he murmured.

Gabby
The Perfect Night

I woke up slowly, peaceful, in the soft, silver evening light coming through the picture window of the most intimate bedroom I'd seen in my life. Nest, hideaway, sanctuary, haven. The sheets were softly textured silver flannel; the air, sweet with roses in a vase on an old table by one stone wall. The light toasted the filmy drapes an eggshell color.

This was a bedroom made to be shared by a couple who had no secrets. I felt the bedroom's effect in my thighs, my breasts, my womb; Jay's hands and lips and *other,* even though I was alone. The pulse of him, inside me. I'd fallen asleep fully dressed, alone. But with his kiss on my forehead and his hands tucking the covers around me.

They ate apple pie and ginger ale spiced with peach schnapps, here. I taste . . . honey and hot biscuits; also the hard-sweet bite of smooth corn whiskey and passion. Caillin and John.

The bed was huge, with tall, carved posts; a downy nest of flannel, embroidered linens, quilts and a thick comforter. Across from the foot, a large picture window framed the snowy horizon of the Eerie Gal mountains. A magenta slash of color hooded their setting sun in a sea of pewter clouds. To my right, a large wooden door with a stained-glass transom was carved with Celtic eternity symbols and a stylized oak tree. One of the valley's legendary Memory Oaks. Above a lovely old side table, where the roses stood like full red lips, a tall painting took my breath away.

I put my bare feet on a thick fleece rug as soft as a kitten's fur. My hiking boots lay across the room. I was still dressed in sweaty, pickle-stained jeans and a shirt. Rumpled and hypnotized, I made my way to the painting. A small portrait lamp illuminated it from above. There was no name plate, but I knew the man and woman must be Caillin MacBride — my ancestor — and John Bonavendier, of the New Orleans' Bonavendiers, Will's grandfather. Her daughter came from a previous marriage, as did his children.

I studied the tall oil portrait. She and John sat atop one of valley's monolithic granite and limestone outcroppings. They lazed, deceptively casual and sympatico, almost like movie stars camping in the southern wilds. Both wore slouchy pants and shirts; broad-brimmed felt hats were tilted back on their heads at rakish angles. Her deep auburn MacBride hair tangled in retro waves down one shoulder; his dark brows and somber, craggy face tilted toward hers with affection. His arm was draped around her shoulder; hers was curled around his updrawn knee. A thick wooden cane leaned against his thigh.

He limped. "He had a spinal injury on one side," said Caillin in her journal. *I walked beside him knowingly, careful of his dignity. I told him a man didn't need two perfect legs when he was blessed with angel wings.*

They were in love. Caillin and John seemed larger than life against the background of rounded mountains, cerulean sky, and billowing, gray-white thunderheads. The violence and passion in those clouds filled the painting with drama; even the sky predicted the forces leading to John's death in the valley and accusations of murder against her when she fled. Her body had never been found among the wreckage of the small plane John had taught her to fly. Her plane had gone down in the cold waters beyond North Carolina's Outer Banks. To some, she'd been a seductress, leading her John a merry chase in her bid to regain the Little Finn valley. To others, she was a woman who loved true and hard and without reservation. John had been willing to jeopardize his legacy for her.

The ironies and contradictions echoed in

my own life. *Loyalty is a liquor distilled from love and trust. Grief and revenge can define families for generations to come. Love and devotion can overcome any curse. Or can they?*

He's doomed, Donny had said.

A chill went through me. *No. I can save him.*

I walked into a bathroom, softly lit by a single wall sconce. I took a shower with water warmed by solar panels on a cistern above the cottage roof. On a hanger I saw a short nightgown, unbelievably feminine and flowing, with embroidery of pale silk flowers on the bodice. I put it on. It felt not quite made for me, a midi-length sheath that would have been more classic on a shorter, smaller woman. On me it was a nightie, not a gown. My legs looked pale beneath the hem, a thousand miles long. Too long. Too thick. Not at all like I'd dreamed in fantasy.

Apples and rum. She offered him apple cider mixed with rich, dark rum. After several drinks his hands filtered through this gown to frame her breasts, then trailed down her stomach to her thighs, and he poured the apple-laced liquor between them . . .

This gown had belonged to Caillin. She had been shorter than me, more delicate. I looked at my image in a mirror on a claw-footed stand. My hair tangled around my shoulders and down my back. The soft material clung to my breasts. The embroidered hem whispered around my thighs.

I looked vintage. And sexually aware. The gown was short and nearly sheer.

So be it. Why pretend this was my and Jay's first date?

I opened the bedroom door. The scent and heat and soft crackling of a fireplace came to me. Masculine essences, primitive. At the end of a short hall I pivoted through a small archway. There, amidst crowded bookcases and fat sofas, old lamps and crystal bottles of richly-colored liquors, Jay stretched his long body along a pillowed chair and leather ottoman. A faded flannel shirt and thin chinos draped his powerful chest and legs; his big feet were bizarrely encased in cheerful red and green Christmas socks with a snowman motif.

Those socks made me love him even more.

The smart phone in his big hands seemed . . . cuddled. He held it the way a fatherly man holds a baby. The sight filled my belly with an ache. I knocked on the wall to warn him I was watching. He pretended to keep reading. "You're ogling me," he said.

"It's the socks. I have a thing for yarn snowmen."

"They were sent here, made for me, by Lucy Parmenter. Anna is one of her mentors. 'Women of the eternal yarn,' they call themselves."

"We need to tell Gus about Lucy's history. But Tal says Lucy doesn't want to. She likes being his pen pal, and doesn't want him to feel sorry for her."

"He'll come home someday, on leave. He'll come looking for her. He needs to know."

"How interesting," I said. "You think people who care about each other should be trusted with the facts about their backgrounds and motives."

He raised his eyes to mine. "Let's change the subject. You almost set a world record for pickle eating today." He waggled the phone at me. "Google says so." His baritone, an elegant Asheville drawl with worldly consonants, seeped inside me. Changing the subject. How Jay-like.

I countered. "I can swallow a long pickle without even taking a breath."

His eyes went darker. He set the phone on a table. "Not fair."

I laughed.

He nodded. "Tell me more."

282

Foreplay. This was it.

His dark hair was damp and tousled, forgetting that some expensive private barber had sculpted it in Asheville. His face looked scraped, as if he'd shaved his jaws with a sharpened flint rather than a razor. A tiny fleck of blood high on his cheekbone confirmed he might have been distracted or reckless.

I walked toward him, slowly. "I just . . . slip a pickle into my mouth and . . . bite down. Hard."

"You can't scare me." He raked my sheer gown with a glance that burned my skin. "I'm already distracted."

"Flattery."

He shifted his feet on the ottoman and picked up a tall glass of amber liquid. "Please sit. Here." He held out the glass.

I took the cool crystal cylinder — no ice, neat, a fat double of golden whiskey with the rich scent of fermented grain and Forgetting. I sat down by his Christmas socks from Lucy Parmenter and sipped the smooth liquid. "Wonderful. Apples and cinnamon and corn and honey. A slight acid tang of fermentation. Perfect. Every plant, every bee and farmer and hummingbird and human being who made this. I *feel* them all. How old is this?"

"Anna says it's another bottle from a hidden stash that survived the raid. That Caillin knew where the remnants of the best liquor were stored in the caves and cellars the feds didn't find in nineteen thirty. This whiskey is at least eighty-five years old. It's amazing that it's even drinkable, much less world-class."

The people who grew the corn that made this whiskey are inside me; they lived and loved in this valley, they brewed the mash and distilled the essence and stored it in barrels made from the timbers of their Memory Oaks . . . they're here, in my blood, slipping down my throat, whispering to me in the spirit of this spirit.

"We're sharing it. They want us to."

"Yes."

My hand shook slightly as I leaned over and set the glass on a stone coaster atop the lamp stand. "I need to ask you some questions. Don't dodge them. Gus has already blown your cover."

"Never trust a MacBride. It's a Wakefield motto."

"You've always said it wasn't safe for me to know everything about your business. I want to know what you mean by that."

"Family legacies have a way of re-seeding themselves in every new generation. The stronger the mutation, the more it reinforces a dominant trait. The sad fact is: *my* family's primary trait is the joy of crushing its opposition by any means necessary. Your family's primary trait is resisting the opposition even if it kills them."

"I don't believe that. Your tendencies aren't quid pro quo. Not in your case. And not in your father's."

"I like it when you talk legal Latin to me."

I leaned toward him. Suddenly the short space between us was reduced to a heated transfer of sexual tension. A hot, invisible stream. "If you're going to stonewall me, at least get as naked as I am."

A ripple of response shimmered through him. "What would you suggest?"

"You can see me through this gown. I want to see at least a little more of you. Take off your shirt."

He curved his fingers beneath the rumpled hem then slowly lifted it over his head and dropped it softly to the floor. He was heavier than ten years ago; so was I. The added weight made a firm layer over his well-set chest and abdomen, his thick shoulders and veined forearms. An inverted triangle of dark chest hair led down to his navel. It disappeared beneath the waistband of his pants, where the soft material rode a thick bulge.

An aura of acceptance, of welcome, settled around me. There is a moment when the consummation between lovers is inevitable; the die has been cast; the rest becomes preparation, acknowledged by both parties. Great truths and easy lies simmer in that phase. I hoped for the former.

"What is the danger?" I stroked a finger down the center of his abdomen, pressing my fingernail into his flesh.

He grasped my hand gently and stroked my trapped fingers to his jaw. "That you'll decide you hate my family, and leave me."

Like his mother did.

I curled a fingertip to the edge of his chin. "You're in luck," I whispered. "I'll judge you only by what you do, not by your name. And when I look at you, I'll only see the man I know personally, not the image you show to others. The man I want, right now."

He reached for me.

The rest was as easy as cooking.

Jay
Merry Christmas, with Pickles

I sat back on my naked heels, holding tumblers of whiskey-laced eggnog in both hands above Gabs's nude body, as starlight filtered through the cottage window. I clamped a slice of dill pickle between my teeth. Blueberry jam, thick with seeds and hulls, was smeared on sensitive areas low on my body. There. And there. Also there. Gabs trailed a finger through a delicate spot, making my back flex. She rubbed the jam into her lower lip and tasted it with her tongue.

I dropped the pickle slice between her breasts, like a devoted dog delivering a bone. "Merry Christmas, Pickle Queen. Snack time."

She lifted the slice to her mouth, sucked it as I watched, then bit and slowly swallowed each piece. She sat up, jiggling and dewy. One hand went between my thighs. The other took her glass of eggnog. We clicked our crystal together. "Merry Christmas," she said hoarsely. "Kiss me. With a lot of tongue."

Five minutes later we were licking eggnog off each other.

The best night of my life.

Gabby
A Dark Morning for Christmas

I dozed in Jay's arms, with his big hands moving down my naked back and over the curve of my hips. Then he slept in my arms, his head pillowed on my breasts as I stroked

287

his hair and face. When the pounding and the yelling woke us, my smart phone said three A.M. The sky outside the big window was snowy and starlit. Magical. Christmas.

"Help us, help us," begged a high, young voice. Female. Terrified.

"Stay here," Jay said. He threw on his clothes and headed through the cottage.

Of course, I followed no more than ten seconds behind him.

Arwen shivered in the low light of a solar lamp outside the front door. She wore nothing but baggy pink flannel pajamas, Ugg boots and a striped sock cap. Her hair stuck out beneath, long and tangled, vaguely dark blond but soaked in sweat. A tiny gold stud rode the crease of her left nostril, and another perched over her right eyebrow. Her pink-lidded eyes were huge and blue. A fairy emblem danced on a leather necklace tied snugly around her throat.

She stared up at us, clutching her hands in front of her. Tears pooled in her tired eyes. "Aunt Denoto's gone crazy. She says she's taking Dustin to Mexico and hide him there — even if he doesn't want to go with her. She tried to shoot the Clagg for getting in her way. Donny freaked out and ran. Dustin tried to catch him. She chased them both. Dustin and Donny climbed down the side of Tendril Bald while The Clagg went for more help. Dustin fell and hurt his arm. My brother says he'll jump if she comes down after them." She pressed her shaking hands to her throat. "Please come before things get worse. Please."

Gabby
The Summit at Tendril Bald

Jay, Arwen and I slipped through the snowy forest to the edge of a high "bald," a broad pate of exposed stone like a skull plate in the mountain's head.

"There," Arwen said, whispering and pointing through a fringe of laurel. Ahead of us was a panorama of starry sky and nothingness. We were at the top of a rounded peak in the Derry Fogs, with craggy overhangs and sheer drops that plunged into winter forest and eagle sanctuaries below. My ears had popped twice on the drive up a rutted trail. The last mile, on foot, had been fast, breathy and hard on my legs.

The sight of Denoto scared the hell out of me.

She stood at the apex of the bald with her booted feet braced apart, coatless, her long dark hair straggling around her shoulders. In one hand she carried a large pistol of some kind. With the other she held up a propane lantern. It's powerful glow cast a weird white circle around her, gleaming on the snow and showing where dangerous patches of ice glittered even brighter. The edge of its light ended where the bald plunged downward into starry sky and tree tops.

She raised her chin and shouted hoarsely, "I can outwait you, Dustin! I'm only trying to do what's best! Don't you understand?"

From below the precipice came Dustin's voice, wracked with pain. "Mom, you have to put the gun down and leave! I can't climb up without Donny, and he's terrified of you!"

"I'll jump!" Donny shrieked. "I'll learn to fly! I'll turn into a bat or an eagle!"

Arwen cried softly. "If we don't do something quick, he really will try to fly. Guns scare him to death."

"Stay here, both of you," Jay ordered. "I'm going through the shadows. I'll climb down and get them."

Be careful . . .

He was gone before I had time to whisper the words.

Jay
Past, Present, and Future

I crawled to the edge of a drop-off that stair-stepped down a thousand feet of craggy rocks, wind-carved pines protruding at impossible angles, and dangerous Nothing. The snow-chilled night wind buffeted me. Beneath the stars, a white panorama of forest rose below me, falling away into broad hummocks and deep nooks. A million wild eyes, some living, some only remembering life, watched me. I pulled a small flashlight from my jacket and directed its beam downward.

A good thirty feet below, Dustin and Donny huddled in the alcove of a jutting boulder. When I was sure I was below the rim and could do it without Denoto seeing me, I shined a flashlight down. Dustin held his injured right arm close to his body and looked up at me like a trapped animal, his face, so much like mine when I was young and couldn't hide it, bitter. "Are you on Grandfather's side?" he asked.

"No."

Donny crouched, pale and shaking. "If you come down here, you'll die. I've seen it."

Dustin's eyes narrowed in pain. "Please don't let anything happen to Donny and Arwen. I can handle the family torture.

They can't."

"Nothing's happening to any of you. I'm getting you out of here, and the three of you are coming with me. Permanently. When I have time to explain, I'll make it clear that that's a happy thing. Nothing for you to dread."

Their fortress was a narrow rock ledge dusted with snow and ice. I hunched my shoulders against a bone-deep cold that seeped out of the abyss. *My whole life has felt like this.*

"I'm coming down to your level," I called to the boys.

Gabby

I heard Will's helicopter coming.

"I'm going to distract your aunt," I told Arwen. "Buy Jay and the boys some more time. Stay here, okay?"

She nodded. "Donny was right. You're a nice lady. And Cousin Jay . . ."

"He's on your side. I promise you."

She nodded.

I crept up the mountainside. When I reached the bald, Denoto was still shouting into the starlit sky, telling Dustin how it didn't matter if his cousins were sacrificed, that they were like the wild hogs of the valley, just useless feeders. I eased into the edge of her wildly swinging lantern light. Waiting for the right moment, watching the gun swing in her other hand.

Jay

"I'm going to jump to my death if you touch me!" Donny screeched.

"Donny, get a grip," Dustin ordered, hugging his damaged arm. "Turn off the voices for a sec, okay?"

The wind whipped around us. Behind me was nothing but mountain ridges and Falling Doom. I snagged the collar of Donny's silver-paint-smeared denim coat. My other hand was busy hanging onto the exposed root of a brave old fir tree that stuck out from the mountainside side a wild hair thumbing its nose at a razor blade. I planted both booted feet into the crevice of a ledge just wide enough to keep me, Donny and Dustin from taking a quick re-enactment of the cliff scenes from *Last Of The Mohicans,* which was filmed in these mountains.

I slammed Donny against the rock face. He slumped. "Ouch. Meanie. Mean man. Darth Vader of Wakefields. You're hurting me."

"You want to get your sister and Dustin out of this predicament? Then do what I tell you. If I'd wanted to destroy your crazy butt

I'd have throttled you in Asheville."

"They're all around you. The spirits. They're talking at me. They're saying . . ." His eyes, large and strangely lit by the flashlight I'd jammed into a crevice, stared into a world only he could see. "They say . . . *chocolate ice cream with Reese's Pieces.* What does that mean? But it's good!"

"Focus, Donny. Focus." I shook him lightly. "You climbed down here. You can climb back up."

"Noooo! She'll shoot me! She'll separate me from my sister. We are twins. We are one heart! I'll die! Arwen's the only one who can keep the voices under control. Dustin, help. Dustin. Dustin, help!"

"I'm hurt, dude. I have to trust Cousin Jay. So do you. There's no other choice."

Donny grabbed the front of my jacket. His pale, young face was full of horror. "What happens next? Grandfather will lock us up. We'll never see Mama again. We won't get to go with her to Disney World."

"I swear to you, Donny, that's not going to happen."

His pale eyes flickered, shifted, then settled on me, widening. "You. Oh. My. God. Ohmagod! *You.* You've changed. You're . . . because of her . . . Gabby, it's

294

you! They recognize you! He's home, they're saying. He's here!" He smiled. "They've been trying to tell me, but I didn't understand, before. It's *you they've been waiting for.*" He let go of my jacket and clamped his clammy hands around my face. He lurched forward and smacked a cold kiss on my forehead.

"Keep it together, Donny. Just climb up and stay in the shadows. Don't go toward Aunt Denoto. Head down the mountain into the woods. Arwen's waiting there, with Gabby. I'll help Dustin up, right behind you. And then I'll climb up. I promise you, Donny. I'll protect you and Arwen and Dustin. I swear to you."

He relaxed. Something inside his churning brain, some illusion or angel voice, had given me the live-long-and-prosper seal of approval. He patted my face. "Now I hope you *don't* die," he said.

Well, *that* was progress.

He let go of me and climbed up nimbly.

Gabby

I was face down in the dirty snow with my nose bleeding and Denoto's knee in the center of my back. She pressed down on my spine, digging the breath out of my lungs. She grabbed the back of my hair and shoved my face into the mountaintop's not-so-delicious crust. "Eat that, Pickle Queen."

I spat out the dirt and tried to flip over, but she twisted my arm behind my back and pinned me tighter to the ground. Through the roar of blood in my ears I heard the *whump whump whump* of the helicopter landing.

"Let Gabby go!" a shrill voice yelled. Oh my God. Donny.

Denoto shoved me aside and clambered to her feet. She rushed forward.

I got up and hurried after her. Ahead of us, in the light of lantern she grabbed and held high, Donny stood like a deer frozen by an oncoming train.

"You're the Wicked Witch!" he yelled.

"Donny!" Arwen screamed, from the woods.

The sight of his beloved sister running toward us, and their aunt wildly waving the gun, sent Donny leaping towards Denoto. She stopped cold and aimed at him. A strange little smile crossed her face. I dived for her but was too late.

Jay, however, wasn't.

He shoved Donny out of the way with the speed and agility that had made him a star in college football.

She fired.

The Rush to Asheville

Blood stained a wide portion of Jay's shirt. I held his hand and hunched beside him on the helicopter's rumbling floor. His eyes, a little too calm and empty, frightening me, were trained on mine. "Right here," I kept saying, pointing to my eyes. Don't look away.

He had lost a lot of blood.

Will's people had Denoto under control, and were taking Dustin, Donny and Arwen to a quiet place. Bonnie sat cross-legged on the copter's rumbling floor beside Wren, who had one Latex-gloved hand pressed to Jay's bullet wound. A tuft of tubular cotton protruded from the hole in his chest. Field emergency. A tampon. "Best way to staunch the bleeding," she had murmured.

When Jay recovered, he'd get a laugh out of being plugged with it.

He will recover. He has to.

She put her stethoscope to Jay's bare chest. "ETA?" she asked Will.

"Thirty minutes to Asheville. They're waiting for us on the helipad at the hospital."

"He'll need blood. Fast."

I studied the pallor in Jay's face, and the way his eyes had gone half-shut. I put my face close to his, my lips brushing his cheek.

In a distant part of my brain, my broken nose ached. "Don't leave me. I swear to God, if you do, I'll come after you."

His eyes flickered. His lips moved. I put my ear to them, dreading what he might say.

He said it.

"Love you. Always."

"Don't you dare." I wrung his hand, which was cooling inside my ferocious grip. "I won't hear it! Not this way. I did not hear it! You hear me? You can't say it this way! I know what you're trying to do. You know I love you and the only way you'd leave me is to finally admit you love me too. Don't you leave me! No! Jay. No!"

He shut his eyes.

I bent my forehead to his and prayed to every god I knew.

Gabby
The Long Night of Worry and Love

Eight A.M. Christmas morning. Touch and go. Jay was out of surgery and in recovery. The bullet had nicked an artery. "He's stable," the surgeon said. "For now. The next few hours will tell us more."

Will and Bonnie waited with me, along with George Avery, who never sat down. He paced the floor along with me. "I let him down," George said. "I should have gone with him up there."

"He had to go about this in his own way, George. He doesn't ever like asking for help, not from you, and not from me."

"He is a good man. Like a son to me. I've never told him that."

"I believe he knows it."

"His plan was working. He would have accomplished exactly what he intended. Gotten the kids out of his uncle's control, secured the mineral rights for Free Wheeler permanently, and broken E.W.'s power base once and for all." George stopped, his throat straining. "His plan *is* working. What am I saying? I can't be negative. I'm talking as if . . . Oh, my God."

"Tell me about this plan," I said hoarsely.

"Bit by bit. Suspicious land deals. Bribes. Under-the-table arrangements with politicians. Mining accidents that were hidden from safety regulators. We've always hammered E.W. on all the little things we could find. But the big ones . . . they go so far back that many of the records don't even exist. Courthouses burned down. File clerks lost files. Sometimes they were paid to lose paperwork. Deeds were rewritten. Wills disappeared. Back in the old days . . ."

"How far back?"

"We could go back to the 1920s, but E.W.'s part starts in the late 1960s. He was in his late twenties then."

"Around the time his father gambled away the mining right to Mary Eve Nettie?"

"Yes. It was around that time that E.W. staged a coup and took control of Wakefield Mining. And all its secrets. Some of which had to continue to be . . . tended. Like an old mine that has too many tunnels. You never know when someone will fall down an old shaft or stumble into a forgotten quarry and drown. They still have value — or liabilities. You can't afford to let anyone take control of them and start prowling around, so as long as you remain the owner, you'll always be filling in those old holes, covering up those old secrets."

"He's been involved in covering up crimes committed by his father?"

George nodded. "And grandfather. And great-grandfather."

I stared at him. "Including . . . in the Little Finn . . ."

"That's the heart of it, but actually one of the least he's worried about. The MacBrides ran distilleries. They were famous for their liquor. Respected citizens. Patriots. But when Prohibition came along they refused to quit the business. That wasn't uncommon. There was more liquor made in these mountains during Prohibition than before or after. But it made them a target. It was easy to use that as excuse. What Augustus wanted wasn't just the mineral rights to the valley — he wanted the rights to other properties the MacBrides owned, more valuable ones, including gold, in these mountains. He wiped out an entire generation so that he could take over a dozen mines they owned."

I found a chair and sat down. George lowered himself wearily beside me. "William did everything up to and including murder to keep those mines. E.W. took up where William left off."

"He caused my mother's death — I call that murder, but that's not what you mean, is it?"

He shook his head. "Caillin MacBride. She didn't die in a plane crash."

"You're telling me that E.W., as a young man . . . killed her."

"No." George looked at me evenly, a plain and friendly-faced man, a good man, the kind who expects to deal with ugliness but never doubts that wondrous and even miraculous things exist. "He only *thought* he did."

I paced in front of a window where dawn was warming up to a bright blue Christmas day. Asheville and the mountains looked silver and misty in the rising mists of mountain fog; pristine and yet painfully lonely to me. I limped as I tracked back and forth across a secluded end of the waiting room. Denoto had landed several painful hits on my right knee. My fists were raw. The nurses had given me a green scrub shirt to trade for my bloody sweater, and an ER doc had proclaimed my nose fractured but not "unaligned." Since the bleeding had stopped on its own, he'd simply handed me some acetaminophen for the pain, then backed off as I rushed out.

"When can I see Jay?" I asked as a nurse arrived. She frowned at Charlie, who manned the door as my personal off-duty police security. "Ten minutes. We're getting him settled in intensive care."

Will asked, "Is he conscious?"

She shook her head. "We don't want him to be. He needs to stay quiet for a few hours."

She left, glaring at Charlie again. He gave her a grunt of manly appraisal. He and

Daddy's other old friends could not be dissuaded from setting up shifts as the MacBride family security team. Not only were reporters downstairs trying to sneak up here for inside information on the bizarre incidents of the night, but Denoto was being taken into custody. She needed help.

Suddenly, Charlie lurched down the hall like a happy bear, spreading his arms wide. "Baby Tallulah! Oh my lord, you're a sight for sore eyes!"

I rushed after him. *Tal.* I had never been the teary, clinging one of the family; I was always the oldest girl — the stern, substitute mother, trying uselessly to replace Mama. Her death had been hardest on Tal. I knew that. But now I ran toward Tal as if I were the baby sister and she were Mama and Daddy and Brother Gus rolled into one. She turned from Charlie's bear hug, mewled at the sight of my swollen nose, haunted eyes and limping, bruised-knuckle self, then threw her Christmas-sweatered arms around me and pressed her teary cheek hard against mine. Two big women colliding in an explosion of red hair and freckles.

Behind her, one brawny hand gently touching her back as a sign of support, stood the legendary Dr. Douglas Firth — veterinarian, Tal's knight in shining Scottish plaid, a man who had already proved that he was not only her loving partner but also a devoted father figure for her young daughter — my niece, Eve.

Tal and I swayed, holding each other.

It was good to be home.

"We have to talk," I told her. "It's about Caillin MacBride."

Jay
From the Depths of the Dream

Look at the ocean, Jay. It seems endless and . . . peaceful. Out there beyond the edge of the world. Where the water falls off the edge, into heaven. You and me. Let's go see that waterfall. Together.

I was looking at Gabs's profile as she held my hand, naked, in the gold-pink light of a Malibu sunset. Beautiful, I said.

"We'd hoped for more improvement in his vitals by now. He's in a very deep place. I just want you to understand the challenges. We almost lost him in surgery. The outcome is still unpredictable."

"Thank you," I heard Gabs say to the doctor. "But you don't know him the way I do."

Lips brushed my ear. The scent of soft pickling spices and love filled me. Gabs whispered, "You owe me a visit to that waterfall. Please."

I tried to turn my head toward her, to answer.

But the sunset stood between us like a wall.

Gabby

Three A.M. me and Jay, alone. Now we shared the day *after* Christmas. The night-shift nurses — wise and unflappable ICU veterans — wouldn't meet my eyes when they promised it was just a matter of time before he woke up.

I sat on the bed with my hip against his, cradling his hand on my thigh, and talking to him about everything George had told me. "Do you think you have to die to make up for your family history?" I asked him. "No. You have to live. Anna Shepherd told me that a piece of yarn is made special by the strength of its core. I know what your core is, and it's not your name or your family tree or your money or what happened in the past. It's your heart. You are still that boy who wants the sweetness of chocolate ice cream. Your father was a great man. You've made him proud. My parents loved you. Gus and Tal love you. I love you. You have a family that defines you, and that family is us."

But finally there was nothing to do but

simply say, my voice so hoarse and small with misery that it was a whisper, that I loved him, I loved him, I loved him. That I would never leave him.

Crying silently, I bowed my head and shut my eyes.

His hand flexed inside mine.

He was back.

The Next Day, Onward

Tal and I stepped off Will's copter into the cold air of the Little Finn Valley. He stayed in the pilot's seat, waiting. I wanted to get back to Jay as quickly as possible.

In the middle of the empty street of the town MacBrides had built, Tearmann, Anna leaned on a cane and watched us walk towards her. Her long gray hair wafted in the air; a beautiful shawl of gray wool moved gracefully around her body.

"Apples," Tal whispered. "A whole orchard of them."

I nodded.

I wore the pretty shawl Anna had given me when I arrived in the valley. As we drew closer to her I pulled it off the collar of my coat and held it out across my hands. "Well, now I know where my brother's knitting talent comes from."

Anna smiled. In the bright light, her face

was much, much older. "I'll send him some yarn. Core-spun. We MacBrides like our Wensleydale yarns to last a hundred years. At least."

Her Irish lilt was gone. In its place, a soft Carolina drawl. As we stopped close to her, Tal said, "Is that how old you are? I know it's not polite to ask. Our mama is whispering 'For shame, Tallulah', in my ear, right now."

"Under the circumstances," Anna said, "it's certainly important to be honest. I am ninety-five. I was born in nineteen seventeen, here in this valley. I was thirteen years old when the massacre occurred. On a spring night in April, under a moon we called the shepherd's moon."

"Why have you stayed in disguise all these years, letting E.W. think you died?"

"He accused me of killing John. How John died is a painful story, and E.W. knows it was not my doing. That secret stays with me. But had he framed me for the murder, this valley would have fallen into his hands instead of going to John's family."

"You planned to remain hidden forever?"

Anna nodded. "But now my family has returned. And without my help, Jay's efforts to conquer E.W. will fail." She looked at Tal and I. "I won't fail you. And I won't let Jay's sacrifice mean nothing. This is your home. Yours and your brother's and Will and Bonnie's. I finally understand that the power of what we were is still here. That it has passed down despite all the efforts to destroy it. That this valley, and the heritage here, can be trusted to family that includes, yes, even a Wakefield. A name I never thought I'd utter as an ally."

I put a hand to my heart. "Jay sends you his devotion."

"He suspected my identity for years. If he'd been reckless . . . if he hadn't cared about the consequences for me, for Will and Bonnie and this valley, he'd have used me as a weapon before everything else was in place. But he protected me. He would never have exposed me without my permission. He's a good soul."

"He is," I said.

She leaned heavily on her cane. Tal and I reached for her but she brushed us away. "Nona is standing just yon." She indicated a shop doorway. "She's got something for you. Documents. Recordings. My side of the story. Evidence. Everything George Avery says he'll need to hand to the police."

She looked up at us with faded eyes that went a little dreamy. "I do have a great-granddaughter somewhere. I plan to live long enough to find her. That's another reason I've stayed hidden. I didn't want E.W. looking for my heirs."

"We'll look for her. You know Jay and I will help."

"Of course. But you'll be busy getting married, and enjoying Free Wheeler. There won't be any problem with those mining rights, not with E.W. locked away."

With that, she pivoted gracefully and walked away, her hair moving around her, her gait slow, steady and proud.

"Can you feel all the spirits around her?" Tal whispered.

I could. An entire town, her family, John Bonavendier, they were all with her.

"We'll see you again soon," I called. "Caillin MacBride."

She halted at the sound of that long-unheard name. Her shoulders straightened; her head incline regally in response.

The air seemed to shimmer around her.

Jay
The Time Has Come

It all seemed surreal. Anticlimactic. I lay in a hospital bed with Gabs sitting beside me, Tal and Doug and Will and Bonnie standing or sitting in the room, George and Charlie there, too. Delta and Pike were on the phone from New York, where they had a computer feed to watch the developments unfold along with us. We all watched on computer screens, live, as the police arrested my uncle at his home for the attempted murder of Caillin MacBride. It had taken forty years to put E.W. in jail for any crime at all, much less one that had stunned the city, the state, and even the country. The story of E.W. Wakefield's downfall and the bizarre, Shakespearean history of the Wakefield family made for good gossip. Wakefield Mining and Land Development would fall into the hands of creditors and the few partners E.W. had taken on over the years.

Maybe E.W. would beat the ancient charges against him and get off with a short sentence or none at all; but I doubted it. Either way, the Wakefield name was in ruins. Dustin, Arwen and Donny were in my care, soon to be formal guardianship, God help me, though Gabs was confident we could be good parents to one normal teenager and two elves.

I'd never been happier to be an outcast.

Later, When All Is Quiet . . .
"George?"
"Why are you whispering, sir?"
"Gabs is asleep. Get us out of here before

the nurses catch her on the bed with me, again. The night shift was just happy to see me alive and being cuddled. But the day team wants to follow ICU protocol. Can't blame them, but I want Gabs right where she is, not sleeping in a chair in a corner."

"I'm working on the transfer, sir. And sir, it's so good to hear your voice. Your progress over the past few hours is remarkable, sir."

"George?"

"Yes, sir?"

"Stop calling me *sir*. You're like a father to me. I love you."

Silence. Then: "You . . . what? I think my phone reception is weak."

"I love you, George. I've learned a lot in the past few days. How to almost die. How to live. And to say 'I love you.' "

"They're still giving you narcotics for the pain?"

"*I love you,* George. I'm not going to hesitate to say that to the people I care about, not anymore. But let's not get smarmy about it."

"I love you, too, sir. Like a son. This is awkward. Can we stop, now?"

"Yes."

"I'll have you and Ms. MacBride transported by private ambulance to your loft within the next hour. With private medical staff on hand. I've set up Ms. MacBride's sister and friend in condo. Your cousin Will is in another. Dustin and the twins are being moved to the Crossroads Cove. Sergeant Vance asked to be your escort. There's quite a lot of media. We'll bring you in through the back. The service elevators."

"Thank you. Good job."

"About the pickles. The decorators are finishing up, right now."

"Gabs will love that. I hope."

"She'll love it, yes. Because she loves *you.* Her devotion to you has been unquestionable. Merry Christmas, sir."

"You're backsliding, George."

"Merry Christmas, son."

"Merry Christmas, Pops."

"No! I'm not really old enough to be your father. And I respect the memory of your dad too much to . . ."

"He'd be honored if you'd call me 'son.' And I'd be honored."

"Okay . . . son. What will you call me?"

"Paps?"

"Sounds like a beer."

"Bubba Dadda. Covers two roles."

"How about just 'George?' "

"A deal. I love you, George."

"I love you, son."

Gabby
A Yuletide of Gherkins

This was the man I loved: barely out of a coma after being shot and suffering a near-death experience, but already directing his minions to sweep me off to his private lair in Asheville and help *me* recuperate in the luxury of his manly nest. The trauma of the past several days was a wound we'd both need time to heal.

He's alive. So am I. We're together. Tal and Eve are safe and happy with Doug Firth, and Gus is . . . well . . . following the calling he loves, in the Middle East. Whatever happens next . . . we can handle it.

Jay gave me a thirty-foot-tall Christmas tree.

Made of pickles.

Jars of pickles, that is. All glossy and green, stacked and somehow secured (hot-glued? duct-taped?) into a perfect, cone-shaped pyramid that nearly touched the high ceiling of his loft. The pickle-jar tree winked with expertly filigreed white lights inside its core. I turned off all the lights in the condo's living room. An enormous green bow capped the tree's top. The pyramid of gleaming pickle-liciousness stood before a beautiful backdrop of darkly-wooded French doors that opened onto a balcony overlooking the city.

Stars shown in the sky. A fire crackled in a copper-hooded contemporary fire pit. I sat on a fat, low ottoman next to Jay, who was comfortably stretched out on a leather couch with an IV still in one arm and pillows propping him up. One of Anna's beautiful woven blankets, made at the old mill in the valley, covered him.

We held hands and looked at the wonderfully odd Christmas tree.

"It's a pickle Mona Lisa," I said. "A pickle-jar extravaganza. Tal says Santa Joe built a nativity scene at the Cove out of chain-sawed logs. Maybe next year we can build a pickle nativity?"

"The baby Jesus would be made of kosher dills," Jay said.

I laughed until my bruised face couldn't take it anymore.

By then, he was pulling me to him and kissing the pain away.

AUTHOR'S NOTE

In 2013 we had a rainy season in Georgia that rivaled the monsoons of Kuala Lumpur, thus creating vast jungles where my garden used to be — stunting the sun-loving peppers, rotting the garlic, and inviting legions of slugs to feast on the pathetic survivors of Veggie Land. Despite that, the PICKLES triumphed. (In their pre-pickle state, that is.)

Those cucumbers ruled! I plucked so many cukes by early August I began to transfer hungry slugs to the plants to slow the avalanche. No success. Cukes must give off some kind of slug repellent. Also mouse, crow, raccoon, 'possum and bear repellent. When even 'possums won't steal a veggie off the vine, you know it's a kick-ass plant.

I understand why the art of pickling can be traced back as far as ancient Egypt: during a rainy summer, cucumbers threatened to take over the pyramids. At some point, Cleopatra wandered into a palace kitchen and shouted to her chefs, "Serve me one more cucumber salad, and I'll open up a can of *whup-asp* on you!"

So to my unstoppable cucumbers, and their pickled cousins, I credit the culinary inspiration for this book.

Many thanks to Eileen Dryer for the wound-tampon idea, Deb Dixon for being the wisest, best and most patient editor I've ever had, Hank for loving me even when I stagger to bed at four A.M. muttering "Plot point, plot point," and my entire BBB family for being supportive, not to mention looking the other way when I was sleep-deprived and crabby. And yes, when they read this they will say, "How is that different from usual?"

ABOUT THE AUTHOR

Deborah Smith is the author of more than thirty-five novels in romance and women's fiction, including the *New York Times* best-seller, *A Place to Call Home,* and the *Wall Street Journal* bestseller, *The Crossroads Café.* She is also a founding partner and editorial director of BelleBooks/Bell Bridge Books, a Memphis-based publishing company known for quality fiction and non-fiction by new and established authors. *The Pickle Queen* is the second of *The Crossroads Café* Novellas, spin-offs set in the Appalachian world of *The Crossroads Café.*

Visit Deb at www.deborah-smith.com and www.bellbridgebooks.com. Also on Facebook at Deborah Smith Author.

The employees of Thorndike Press hope you have enjoyed this Large Print book. All our Thorndike, Wheeler, and Kennebec Large Print titles are designed for easy reading, and all our books are made to last. Other Thorndike Press Large Print books are available at your library, through selected bookstores, or directly from us.

For information about titles, please call:
  (800) 223-1244

or visit our Web site at:
  http://gale.cengage.com/thorndike

To share your comments, please write:
  Publisher
  Thorndike Press
  10 Water St., Suite 310
  Waterville, ME 04901